# ABOUT THE AUTHORS

**Leslie Kelly** has written dozens of books and novellas for Harlequin Blaze and HQN. Known for her sparkling dialogue, fun characters and depth of emotion, her books have been honored with numerous awards, including a National Readers' Choice Award, an *RT Book Reviews* Award, and three nominations for the highest award in romance, the RWA RITA® Award. Leslie lives in Maryland with her own romantic hero, Bruce, and their three daughters. Visit her online at www.lesliekelly.com or at her blog, www.plotmonkeys.com.

**Janelle Denison** is a *USA TODAY* bestselling author of more than fifty contemporary romance novels. She is a two-time recipient of the National Readers' Choice Award, and has also been nominated for the prestigious RITA® Award. Janelle is a California native who now calls Oregon home. She resides in the Portland area with her husband and daughters, and can't imagine a more beautiful place to live. To learn more about Janelle, you can visit her website at www.janelledenison.com, or you can chat with her at her blog, www.plotmonkeys.com.

Over the course of her career, *New York Times* and *USA TODAY* bestselling author **Julie Leto** has published more than forty books—all of them sexy and all of them romances at heart. She shares a popular blog—www.plotmonkeys.com—with her best friends Carly Phillips, Janelle Denison and Leslie Kelly, and would love for you to follow her on Twitter, where she goes by @JulieLeto. She's a born-and-bred Floridian homeschooling mom with a love for her family, her friends, her dachshund, her lynx-point Siamese and supersexy stories with a guaranteed happy ending.

# Leslie Kelly
# Janelle Denison
# Julie Leto

## THE GUY MOST LIKELY TO...

**HARLEQUIN**®

entertain, enrich, inspire™

ISBN-13: 978-0-373-79698-4

THE GUY MOST LIKELY TO...

Copyright © 2012 by Harlequin Books S.A.

The publisher acknowledges the
copyright holders of the individual works
as follows:

UNDERNEATH IT ALL
Copyright © 2012 by Leslie Kelly

CAN'T GET YOU OUT OF MY HEAD
Copyright © 2012 by Janelle Denison

A MOMENT LIKE THIS
Copyright © 2012 by Book Goddess, LLC

Recycling programs
for this product may
not exist in your area.

www.Harlequin.com

**Printed in U.S.A.**

# CONTENTS

# LESLIE KELLY

**UNDERNEATH IT ALL**

To Janelle and Julie. This project has been
a long time coming...I'm so thrilled we got to
work together at last! Long live the Plotmonkeys!

# Prologue

*The Winfield Academy Times*
*May 2002*
*Prom Rocks: But Where Was The King?*

THIS YEAR'S PROM WAS a huge success!

Held at the downtown Marriott, the members of the class of 2002 partied the night away in their tuxes and glittering dresses. The decorating committee's "A Night in Paris" theme was a big hit and made everyone feel like they were strolling along the Seine or posing for pictures beneath the Eiffel Tower.

Deejay "Mad Mike" spun all the class's favorite tunes, and students and faculty alike shook their stuff on the dance floor. The hotel-catered food was delicious, the punch managed to go all evening without being spiked and everyone had a great time.

There was only one incident, which left prom-goers whispering and confused.

What happened to Prom King Seth Crowder?

His queen—and longtime girlfriend—Lauren Desantos had to go up on the stage alone to be crowned, and her tears sure didn't look like happy ones. Rumor has it that Seth stood

Lauren up, with only a mysterious phone call to explain his absence.

The plot thickened Monday when word got out that Seth had withdrawn from Winfield Academy...and he hasn't been seen or heard from since.

Which begs the question: Where'd he go?

One thing's for sure—judging by the picture of Lauren up on that stage, all alone, looking absolutely heartbroken, Seth Crowder has some explaining to do!

# 1

*Present Day*

STANDING AT THE BACK of the A–E line at the registration desk, her dark sunglasses shielding her eyes and her stiff posture discouraging communication, Lauren Desantos came to a sudden realization. The Marquis de Sade had invented the high school reunion. Him, or that Torquemada guy from the Spanish Inquisition.

It made perfect sense; there could be no other explanation. Only someone who enjoyed seeing others squirm in discomfort, who got off on inflicting pain, who thrived on reducing mature adults back to their overemotional, whiny, bitchy, competitive, miserable adolescent selves, would have thought this reunion thing was a good idea.

As if that wasn't bad enough, along with the fear and discomfort came other remnants of high school days—nervous twitches, weak, fake-sounding laughter. Heck, even long-left-behind acne seemed to show up. It was probably brought about by the stress of wondering who you were going to run into first, who looked better than you did, who would notice the extra ten pounds you'd put on since graduation, who would remember you had once slipped on mashed potatoes in the cafeteria. And, more important, who would ask if you ever fulfilled your dream of becoming a magazine editor and what they would say if they found out you worked in marketing for a grocery store chain.

Yeah. Pure hell. Straight evil. Really, only a masochistic idiot would ever agree to attend one of these reunions.

*So what on earth am I doing here?*

There were a thousand ways she could be spending this lovely summer weekend, including staying with her family during this all-too-rare visit back to the Chicago area. Instead, she'd driven outside the city to this sprawling, dubiously themed hot spot called Celebrations, which catered to the let's-relive-past-glory-days-and-pretend-we-aren't-bitterly-crushed-by-the-reality-of-our-adult-lives crowd. In other words, a reunion resort.

Blech. Next thing you knew, they'd be opening a spot for post-hemorrhoidal-surgery patients to get together and shake their recently-operated-upon backsides.

*So get out. Go before anybody sees you.*

She considered it, but knew she wouldn't. Lauren couldn't disappoint her oldest friend, Maggie, who had been there for her during some rough times. Now, when her friend was so unhappy and lonely after her recent divorce, how could Lauren let her down? She wasn't a coward, or a quitter, so she just had to suck it up and get through this weekend no matter what.

She inched closer to the front of the line, staying quiet, hoping not to be seen by any of the former classmates ahead of her. Some de Sade descendant had decided nobody could get their room key until they checked in at the reunion registration desk. She had fully planned to go to her room and get cleaned up before risking running into anyone, but instead, she got stuck standing here with her suitcase and her messy hair, trying to remain invisible.

The odds weren't good that she'd stay unnoticed. Every

minute somebody recognized somebody else and the squealing commenced. Watching air kisses between girls who had ripped each other to gossipy shreds ten years ago, and man hugs between former jocks whose beer guts now got in the way of a good old-fashioned chest bump, she could only hope the first person to ID her wasn't kissy or bumpy.

"Hello, Lauren."

*Or him.*

Oh, God, she would take kissy, bumpy, fake, shrill, sexist, knowing, biting, sarcastic or slobbering over the voice she'd just heard from directly behind her.

Seth's voice.

*How can this be happening?*

"You're not supposed to be here," she said, still staring straight ahead, not turning her head so much as an inch. Surprisingly, she didn't stammer, sounding in control. She couldn't imagine how that was possible, considering her throat felt filled with a huge, anger-flavored lump.

"Was that why you decided to come?"

"Yes." The one condition she'd imposed on Maggie was that Seth not be attending. As of yesterday, his name hadn't been on the list of attendees. Obviously he'd decided at the last minute to crash. "Still have a problem with that RSVP thing, huh?" *Showing up when he wasn't supposed to, bailing out when he was.*

"Honest as ever, huh?"

His voice was still smooth, easy, sexy and masculine. Just like it had been when he was joking, flirting, whispering sweet words in her ear…and breaking her heart.

Hopefully the rest of him had changed and he had become one of those overweight, prematurely balding, red-nosed-from-too-much-beer guys. Because if he got to keep the delicious voice, he ought to at least have been forced to give up his damn good looks. And maybe a few teeth. And all his hair.

A limb might not be stretching it, either. Or his peni... *Don't even go there.* She wouldn't even allow herself to think about certain body parts and Seth in the same brain wave. Allowing them to come together would be like crossing the beams and disrupting the whole space-time continuum or something.

Needing to know either way, she swung around to face him.

"Oh, hell, you *would* be gorgeous."

Had she said that out loud? Yikes, the way his brow shot up told her she had. "So you were hoping I'd be a total dog?"

"It would only have been fair for your looks to match your character."

He winced. "Score one for Desantos."

"I'm not keeping score," she insisted.

She didn't want to keep score with him, or to exchange zingers. She wanted to go on believing she was completely over him... Which was easier to do when she didn't have to look at his unfairly handsome face.

The eighteen-year-old Seth had been super cute in the way young, lean guys are. The twenty-eight-year-old one ought to have one of those hazard labels, like the kind on the side of cigarette packages. *Warning: Guys This Hot Are Dangerous To Your Heart and Your Underwear.*

Because he was so very, *very* hot. He'd break hearts and melt panties. Seth was a veritable perfect storm of good looks and sexuality, designed to sink a woman's resistance and drown her in her own physical hunger.

His hair was thick and dark, shorter now, but he had a few of those tiny finger-tempting curls at his nape. The dark green eyes were deep-set, heavily lashed, punctuated by light laugh lines on either side, and they still twinkled. *Ugh.*

His face was a little scruffy, unshaven. No more smooth-cheeked youth, he had the kind of rough jaw a woman would want rubbing against her skin, leaving deliciously wicked red marks.

And his body…wow, the body had definitely matured. Seth had played football in high school, but he'd been the quarterback, so he'd been fast and lean, not bulky. Now he had muscles on top of his muscles. Every inch of him looked powerful, from the broad shoulders clad in a tight black T-shirt down to the massive chest, the rippled stomach with hair…

*Stop it. You can't see his stomach or any hair.*

Only, she could. In her mind's eye.

She suddenly realized he'd caught her staring. Heat rushed into her cheeks. Jeez, she hadn't blushed since she was a teenager.

"So, do I pass inspection?"

"Not even close."

"Why do I get the feeling you were wishing I'd be bald and covered with scars from a virulent case of shingles?"

"You're too young for shingles. Chicken pox would have suited me fine," she said with a smirk. "I bet you'd be a scratcher."

"Why do you say that?"

"Because you were always ready to scratch your itch the minute it started to bug you," she replied, remembering his rep as a player from when she'd first started school with him in their junior year.

"As I recall, I was kept unscratched and uncomfortable for a pretty long stretch there before graduation."

She ignored the implication. "What would *you* know about graduation?" He hadn't shown up there, either.

"Touché. By the way, it's nice to see you, too," he said, his grin widening, fully aware she was angry about finding him every bit as sexy as she'd hoped, as hot as she'd prayed he *wouldn't* be.

"*Nice* isn't exactly the word I'd use."

Ignoring her, he took a long second of his own to look her over, from top to bottom, and Lauren sent up a mental curse against the person who'd designed airplane seats to be tiny and clothes-rumpling, and their processed air to be hair-flattening and makeup-melting. Of course it hadn't helped that a harried mommy and her way-too-big-to-be-a-lap-baby demon spawn had been seated beside her. The kid kept throwing tantrums and lollipops, one of which had landed in Lauren's hair, which now probably had a sticky streak of red mixed in with the golden brown. And the little brute had been a kicker, so she had a bruise on the side of her arm.

*Worst. Day. Ever.*

Okay. Nix that.

*Second. Worst. Day. Ever.*

He stared at her, as if he couldn't look enough, and Lauren found herself shifting from foot to foot, like a nervous kid being inspected by the school principal.

Good grief, she so needed to get away from this reunion. She was degenerating back to high school mode, even in her thoughts! It didn't help that she suddenly remembered the secret Senior Class Superlatives that had made their way around campus, outside of the safe, sanctioned ones in the yearbook. Seth had been voted "Most Likely to Score with the Prom Queen." She'd forgotten all about it until right now…when she was face-to-throat with the potent male who was supposed to have been her first lover.

It was one more thing to be mad at him for. Because of Seth, she'd lost her virginity to a guy she didn't even like much. Being abandoned by her first love had made her anxious to prove herself worthy of sexual desire, so she'd gone to bed with the first guy she'd dated in college.

He'd thought her clitoris was inside her belly button.

"What are you doing here, Seth?" she finally asked.

"Last time I checked, I was part of the class of '02."

"You didn't show up at graduation," she reminded him again.

"That doesn't mean I didn't get a diploma."

Well, that was news to her.

"I got them to mail it to me," he continued. "I had the grades, even without being there to take my finals."

He'd definitely been smart enough, which had been part of his appeal. Handsome, athletic, sexy and supersmart. Could any girl have resisted him? Certainly none back in high school. He could have had anyone he wanted…but he'd sworn he only wanted her.

They had gone to an exclusive, pricey private school in Chicago. She'd been a scholarship commuter kid from a blue-collar neighborhood who took a city bus to and from classes every day. He'd been a golden boy, a blue blood, living in the Ivy League–priced dorms, occasionally mentioning a family estate outside the city, but mostly not talking about his parents, with whom he didn't get along.

She and Seth had been as different as chocolate and sauerkraut…yet those ten months they'd been together, she'd believed there was nobody else on the planet as right for her.

*Stupid teenager.*

"Did they mail your diploma to the dark side of the moon?" she asked with a sweet smile. "I mean, I assumed you were kidnapped by aliens, the way you disappeared."

"You can't know how badly I feel about that."

"Save it."

"It *killed* me not to be able to take you to prom."

"Yeah, well, believe me, if you'd been close and I'd had a weapon that night, I would have happily taken care of that killing thing for you."

"Lauren…"

"Then, on Monday, when I found out you'd withdrawn from school, I stopped hating you long enough to be *really* worried," she admitted, though she chided herself for the note of concern she still heard in her voice.

But she had been concerned. Concerned enough to forgive him, enough to think something truly awful must have happened. Enough to decide to be there for him during whatever calamity must have befallen him. She'd waited for him to reach out to her to explain. And she'd waited.

Finally, she'd called—number disconnected.

She'd written—letter returned to sender.

Only the fact that his younger sister, a middle schooler, had also withdrawn the same day convinced her Seth hadn't been murdered. That, and his second call. He'd phoned her house that autumn, saying he was okay, and he was sorry.

Lauren had already been living in Georgia with her aunt, having just started her freshman year of college, and her parents had refused to give Seth her number. When her mom called to give her the message, Lauren had only cried for about ten minutes before going back to her regularly scheduled plan of get-over-Seth-and-move-on. End of contact. Until today.

"Lauren, I…"

"Hey, look guys, it's Seth and Lauren! The king and queen of the prom are finally together!"

"Oh, fuck my life," she muttered under her breath.

Seth's quick, short bark of laughter told her she hadn't been quiet enough.

Never had Lauren so wished for a time machine—she'd get in it and go back ten minutes, to the moment when she'd pulled up her rental car in front of this overly lavish place. Instead of parking, she'd have kept on driving. Canada was nice this time of year. Or Mexico. The Sahara. Anywhere else.

Though, honestly, if she had a time machine, she'd be better off going back to warn her young, vulnerable self to never say yes to Seth Crowder in the first place. She could even take an extra minute during the trip to offer herself a stock tip: *Starbucks, yes. Borders, no. Oh, and since you're single, cruise on up to Harvard and introduce yourself to this dude named Mark Zuckerberg. He's single right now, too. He's a bit of an egghead, but he's got an idea for this thing called Facebook…*

"Pose for a picture guys—the one you never got on prom night!"

"Fat chance," she snapped, turning quickly. They could take a picture of her butt as she walked away.

"Lauren, we need to talk," Seth said.

"No, we don't."

"Please!" He held out a hand and put it on her arm.

She shivered slightly, affected in spite of herself. Seth was here, looking at her with desperate longing in his beautiful green eyes, touching her with those strong hands that had once given her as much pleasure as a girl could get with her hymen still intact. This man had been born understanding a woman's anatomy—no belly button confusion for him. He and her clitoris had made friends on their third date. By the fifth they'd been drinking buddies.

But it didn't matter.

"Let me go, Seth," she told him.

"Can't you give me a chance to explain?"

"Nope."

"Come on, a half hour, that's all I ask."

Considering she was already standing here thinking about her panties and her girlie bits, and his habit of making them sing, five minutes was already too long.

"It's not going to happen."

"Why not?"

She answered the only way she could. Truthfully.

"Because I have spent the past ten years either crying over you or hating your guts. I'm over the crying, and I'm past the hating. Now all I feel for you is…nothing. And I intend to keep it that way."

Then, ignoring the wide eyes of their audience, and the tiny gasp of what might have been dismay that he didn't try to hide, she stalked through the lobby and back out the front door of this dubiously named resort.

"Celebrations," hell. They ought to call it "Nightmares."

WELL, THIS WAS GOING to be harder than he'd thought.

Seth hadn't expected Lauren to welcome him with open arms, or to smile and melt against him the minute he looked her way. He had never imagined it would be easy to get her to give him another shot, if not romantically, at least in friendship. Not that friendship was what he really wanted from her. But reconnecting in *any* way was better than the decade of silence he'd just endured.

Still, he hadn't expected the sweet, funny, sexy girl he'd known to tell him she hated him. That stung; he hadn't even known Lauren was capable of that emotion. Then again, she didn't look like the girl he'd known, either. The pretty, vivacious cheerleader had turned into a stunning woman. Her hair was still thick and golden-brown, with highlights that framed her face. Her eyes were still a stunning ice-blue. But the rest of her was all grown-up, intoxicating woman.

"I'd call that being let down hard," said a commiserating voice.

Glancing over, he saw his kid sister, Emily, who had convinced him to come this weekend. Em worked for Celebrations, and she was the one who'd confirmed for him that Lauren would be attending. He hadn't even bothered to let the organizers of the event know he was coming. He just came. Heck, he'd skipped out on prom and graduation, why not crash the reunion?

"Ya think?"

"You knew this wouldn't be easy."

"Nothing ever is," he muttered. And it hadn't been, for a long time. Not since the day of his senior prom, when his entire world had fallen apart.

"You've got the whole weekend. You'll find a way to make her listen."

"And if I don't?"

Emily squeezed his arm. "Then she doesn't deserve you."

"Dude, you got served!" someone else said. The voice was familiar—as was the chortle.

"How's it going, Boogie?" Seth replied with a weary sigh as the other man walked over. He wished he'd followed Lauren out the door. But there wasn't much chance of avoiding the rest of his former classmates in his quest to finally make things right with Lauren, so he figured he might as well get the greetings over with. Besides, he had a few old friends to whom he owed apologies and explanations. Nobody as much as Lauren, but she hadn't been the only one he'd disappointed with his disappearance all those years ago.

The other man—never a close friend—cast him a sheepish glance. "Hey, keep the Boogie on the down-low, man, my wife's over there and she doesn't know that was my nickname."

*Does she know you used to pick your nose and flick boogers on girls in our freshman biology class?*

By their senior year, Billy "Boogie" Drake had liked to pretend he'd earned the name because of his mad dancing skills. *Seriously, Boogie? Did we go to school in, like, 1978?* Of course not. And anybody who'd known him since middle school knew the true origin of the unattractive nickname.

*What the hell am I doing here?* He could be home in L.A., hobnobbing with his clients, some of the wealthiest, most successful athletes in the country.

Then he thought about Lauren—the picture Emily had

shown him of her standing alone on the stage at prom, with the crown on her head—and knew.

He was here to apologize, to explain. To gain forgiveness.

And maybe to see if there was any chance at all of something sparking between them again. Because, as crazy as it sounded, she was his Achilles' heel. Sure, he'd dated plenty of women over the years, some seriously, but Lauren was the one he'd never completely gotten over.

He'd loved her at eighteen. Really loved her, even though, at the time, he probably hadn't quite understood what a momentous thing that was. Now, at twenty-eight, having never loved anyone else, he got it. If only he could get *her*.

"Dude, I can't believe Lauren Desantos didn't spit in your face. I'll never forget how she looked on prom night. Harsh!"

"I heard."

"What the hell happened? You, like, dropped off the face of the earth! We thought you got busted or deported or something."

Seth and his sister exchanged a glance, both undoubtedly thinking the same thing. Busted and deported—that wasn't *too* far off the mark. But he didn't owe those details to Boogie, he owed them to Lauren. And one way or another, he was going to get her to sit down and listen to them.

"Long story," he said.

"Well, you should probably go see if they'll take you as a walk-in," Emily said, pushing him toward the front of the now-empty A–E line in which Lauren had been waiting. Then she whispered, "You're both in the Homecoming Tower, your room's about six doors down from hers, number 1424."

Homecoming Tower? Was it next to the Old Gym Wing and the Principal's Office Ballroom? *Gag me.*

"See you at the dinner tonight…or tomorrow at the carnival?" Boogie asked.

Seth lifted a brow. "Carnival?"

"It's one of Celebrations' specialties," Emily explained. "We have a whole graduation carnival set up on the grounds."

He wondered if it had been his sister's suggestion. She'd been a *Grease* nut in middle school, with the school carnival at the end being her favorite scene. Personally, Seth had always wondered why the cute girl had to turn into a tramp to get the dude.

"There are rides, games," she continued. "Everybody loves it."

Thinking about it, he recalled there had been a carnival at their school many years ago. A fall one, complete with pumpkins, scarecrows and hayrides. He and Lauren had ridden the rides together, already the "power couple" of the senior class…a good seven months out from Seth's family's date with disaster.

He wondered if she remembered. More importantly, he wondered if she'd be there, or if she'd walked out the door, gotten into her car and left altogether.

He didn't think she had. Lauren was furious at him, but she'd never been a coward. When she calmed down and let herself accept the fact that he was here, she'd probably come back ready to tell him off, having thought of a dozen zingers to fling at him.

He could hardly wait to hear them. Because at least it meant she'd be talking to him.

Keeping that thought in mind, he quickly registered, saying hello but not getting involved in any deep conversations. None of his few close friends from high school had checked in yet, which gave him time to go to his room and clean up for tonight's dinner. Tomorrow would be a formal dance—*prom for adults? God, at least there will be booze*—but tonight was a more casual event in one of the private banquet rooms.

Not wanting to risk running into Lauren en route to the dinner, for fear she'd then skip it, he left his room a half hour before it was scheduled to start. He figured he'd kill some time in one of Celebrations many lounges—he'd seen a list of the themed places in his resort guide.

He'd taken a half-dozen long strides toward the elevator, his eyes on her closed door, when he saw that door begin to swing inward. Almost stumbling, he came to a sudden stop.

Praying it was a maid leaving after delivering some extra towels, he held his breath, spying a swish of pink fabric and a delicate bare foot.

Lauren. It had to be Lauren.

He was about to be busted as a freaking stalker.

## 2

"OH, SHIT," SETH MUTTERED. It looked like it was game over. If she found out they were staying on the same floor in this massive place—which couldn't possibly be an accident—not only would she not go to the dinner, she'd probably change rooms. Or leave the reunion altogether.

Not thinking about it, he leaped into a small alcove, trying to cram himself between a small decorative table and the wall. On the table stood a huge vase filled with plate-size flowers, peacock feathers and curly sticks of wood. As he tried to shove himself into the pretty pathetic hiding place, he accidentally set the vase in motion. Lunging, he grabbed the thing in both hands and yanked it toward his chest, hoping not only to steady it but to try to hide behind its fronds and branches.

*This is ridiculous.*

He was acting like...a high schooler. No, worse, a middle schooler, a stalker-y, wimpy kid being led around by his hormones, hoping to make a girl like him. Jesus, he was Seth Crowder, successful sports agent, named as one of L.A.'s most eligible bachelors in a West Coast magazine last year. Yet around Lauren Desantos, he'd become an absolute basket case. This reunion thing was taking all his rational brain cells and mashing them to bits.

"I see you there, you moron."

Gritting his teeth, he peered through the flowers and feathers, imagining the image he presented. Lauren was standing a few feet away, glaring at him, her arms curled protectively around an empty ice bucket. She wasn't yet dressed for the evening. All she wore was a long robe—silky and pink against her skin.

He shoved away the *want, want, want* that filled his brain. "Uh, hi."

"Doing a little redecorating for the hotel?"

He pushed the vase back to the center of the table, then stepped out of the alcove. "I bumped into it and thought the vase was going to tip over."

"So you leaped *behind* the table to steady it?"

Totally busted, he couldn't prevent a self-deprecating grin from widening his mouth. "Would you believe I was trying to steal the flower arrangement? It would go so well with my color scheme."

She snorted. "Not only are you the world's worst decorator, you're one step short of color blind. How did you get my room number?"

No point in denying it. "My sister."

Her brow went up in surprise. "Emily's here?"

Lauren had always liked his kid sister, and had been good to her. She'd taken the five-years-younger girl under her wing and treated her like her own sibling, as if knowing how badly Em needed an older female figure in her life. God knows their mother had never been a good one.

"Yeah, she works at this place."

Lauren's expression turned wistful for a moment. "I'd love to see her," she admitted. Then, as if noticing how much that idea pleased him, she hurried to add, "To tell her to keep customers' room numbers private!"

"Don't be mad at her. You know she always loved us as a couple back then."

She rolled her eyes. "Thirteen-year-olds love Edward and Bella as a couple, too."

"I'm not a vampire."

She hesitated, as if ready to argue that point. She had, after all, already called him a dog and a moron. What was a little *you disgusting bloodsucker* between old friends?

"Well, you sure don't glitter" was all she finally said.

"And you're not a vapid klutz."

One brow arched up. "Do a lot of vampire-romance reading these days?"

He shrugged. "What can I say? Channel surfing on late-night cable."

"Huh. I'd have figured you more for the porn type when you're doing your late-night channel surfing."

*Zing.*

He cleared his throat. Not to mention clearing his mind of the images her words elicited. Porn and sex weren't something he should be thinking about while Lauren was around, not if he wanted to retain his sanity and his edge, both of which were pretty shaky right now. Damn, but the woman could cut the legs right out from under him…and make him laugh while doing it.

"Back to Emily," he insisted. "She loved you. She always wanted you to be her sister-in-law."

Another unladylike snort preceded her response. "Oh, and I suppose you're here to propose to me now?"

*If I did, would you say yes?*

No, of course she wouldn't. Nor was he here to ask that question. Getting her forgiveness and understanding was the first step, maybe dinner and drinks after that. He'd be lucky to get her to voluntarily touch him. Marriage seemed like a distant dream.

Funny, it *had* been what he'd dreamed about all those years ago when he'd been so suddenly separated from her.

Would she believe that?

Probably not.

He stepped closer, unable to resist leaning in to breathe some of that Lauren air. She wore a different perfume than she had in the old days. No longer innocent and flowery, it was heady, womanly, evocative.

Or maybe that was just her. She was incredibly womanly, amazingly sexy, from the top of her shining gold-brown hair down to the tips of her red-tipped toenails peeping out from beneath the robe. And, of course, everywhere in between.

The in-between was especially distracting. Beneath that pink silk was nothing but luscious female. Even with the ice bucket in front of her, he could see the way the V-neckline of the robe revealed some amazing cleavage. Lauren had been more slender as a teenager. Now she was all curves, all inviting and sultry, with full breasts, a small waist and hips that were meant to be clutched in a man's hands. All that, wrapped up in a pink package he wanted to open like a Christmas present.

"Stop staring at me," she said, her voice weak, breathless. As if even she wasn't sure she meant it.

"I can't help it," he admitted. "You're beautiful."

Unable to stop himself, he moved closer, until his shoes nearly touched her toes. The robe flitted against his pants and he caught a glimpse of pale, soft leg.

Groaning low in his throat, he lifted a hand and slid it onto her hip. Memories flooded him, thoughts of how he'd like to encircle her waist in his hands and pull her close now. He'd brush his fingertips along the top curves of her bottom, teasing her lightly, knowing the caresses drove her mad. He would hold her like this, and pull her hard against him to kiss her until neither of them could even think.

She looked up at him, her blue eyes sparkling, and time fell away. Electricity sparked between them and for a half a second, Seth thought she might not punch him if he kissed her.

He leaned closer, needing to taste her. Needing to revisit that place where need and desire and emotion twirled into a quiet storm that both excited and fulfilled.

Their mouths met, a soft brush of lips, a quick tumble into memory, a time when they knew, without a doubt, they were meant to be together.

She tasted like heaven. Like sweetness. Like coming home.

And then she pushed her ice bucket hard against his chest and shoved him back. "That was way out of line."

His hand dropped to his side. His fingers were tingling and hot, already missing the connection, and his mouth ached with the need to taste her more fully, to lick her tongue and plunge his deep, claiming her again.

"Sorry," he said, not really meaning it.

"Just go away, would you?"

He would…except for the fact that his hand and her bucket-fumbling had done some damage to her robe and the thing was now practically gaping open. It was all he could do not to start drooling on the spot as the fabric played peekaboo with one perfect nipple, dark and puckered against the silk.

"And leave you like this?" *Aroused? Unsatisfied?*

"You're acting like I'm half naked."

Fortunately for him, she *was* half naked. He could stand here looking at her all day…or until she moved the bucket again.

Unfortunately, she was half naked in a public hallway. Where anyone else—any other dude—could walk up and see her. They were within eyeshot of the elevators. The doors could slide open at any moment exposing her to the leering eyes of a dozen ex-football players, drunk and horny, wanting to relive their high school carousing.

His inner caveman rising up as he imagined it, he frowned and took her arm. "Let's go into your room and talk in private."

"We have nothing to talk about, and I need some ice," she insisted. Yanking away, she turned toward the vending area, which was right across the hall from the alcove where he'd hidden. At least she hadn't been planning to hike down a long corridor in such skimpy attire.

But that yank and the quick turn made her robe flare even more, from the waist down. It was quick, just a second, then it settled back into place. Even a second was long enough to confirm what he'd suspected: she wasn't wearing one damn thing else. Hunger flooded his mouth and blood roared through his veins, settling right in his groin. His head spinning, his mind tried to re-create the gorgeous, perfect image that had flashed before his eyes.

He was doing an excellent job of it, if he did say so himself. He'd always been a pretty visual guy.

But when he heard a door close from down the hall, Seth reacted quickly. He'd be damned if any other man would get such a gift. Not if he could help it.

He snatched the ice bucket from her hands. "I'll get the stupid ice. Get in your room before some horny creep sees you like this."

"Too late," she said with a sneer.

Oy. Why the hell was he doing this? It would be less difficult to climb Everest than to think Lauren was going to forgive him. And less painful to gnaw his own foot off to get out of a bear trap than endure her insults while he tried to get her to.

"Please, Lauren, get inside," he insisted, gesturing down her body. "That robe might have felt demure when you put it on, but considering your nipples are hard and your legs are shaking, you look like you're begging somebody to do you like you've never been done before."

Gasping, she gripped the edges of the robe and crossed her arms over her chest. "That was…"

"True."

"Damn you, Seth."

"Damn me all you want. Behind closed doors."

She hesitated for a moment, then slowly nodded and turned toward her door, which presented him with the back view— *Good God, that ass is a work of art.* Recently, his memories had been mostly about how much he'd cared about her, loved her, so he hadn't really anticipated such intense heat. It churned in his gut, sucking his breath from his lungs, emptying his brain. He was aware of nothing except her smell and her softness. And how she looked. Oh, God, the way those long, milky-white thighs had looked, topped with a soft tuft of curls he was dying to explore, with his hands, his mouth, his cock. All of the above, once and then again and again.

Every masculine fiber of his being was ready to do it, from his tingling fingertips, to his breathless mouth, to his rock-hard dick, which was currently putting his zipper through one hell of a strength test.

He'd never been so confused by his own emotions. He was torn between anger, regret, excitement and sharp, pounding lust. All directed at or caused by her.

*Get her alone. Say what you have to say. Then see what happens.*

Maybe he'd fly back to L.A. filled with all those same crazy emotions and that same twisted sense of pain and pleasure he felt every minute he spent with her. Or maybe he wouldn't. Maybe she was protesting so much because she still had feelings for him, too.

She might claim to hate him, but once they were alone

inside that room, would the ice queen's facade melt? God, he hoped so.

Hardly able to stand the few minutes more, he watched as she unlocked her door and stepped inside. Then she turned and looked at him. He should have known by her expression she was going to say something he didn't like.

And she did.

"Funny. I've suddenly decided I prefer my water warm." With a triumphant smile, she slammed the door in his face.

*Well, so much for melting.*

"You could give the Snow Miser a run for his money."

He only hoped he wasn't the one who'd frozen her heart into such solid rigidity. God, did he ever hope that.

Seth considered leaving the ice chest right outside her door. It would serve her right if she tripped over it when she left her room. Then he thought better of it, imagining her tripping over the thing, breaking a leg. While he felt aggravated that she was being so stubborn, not giving him a chance to make a proper apology, he didn't want her hurt. Not by him. He'd been there, done that and never wanted to buy another Seth-broke-my-heart T-shirt.

So, filling the bucket with ice for her, and leaving it on the alcove table, he boarded the elevator. He headed for the Wild West saloon-themed bar and ordered a beer. Nursing it, he argued with himself about what he was doing, trying to persuade himself to give up, get a cab to the airport and get on the first plane back to L.A.

But he couldn't. He'd come this far, and had been so close—close enough to touch her, smell her, share her warmth and hear the voice that haunted his dreams. No, he wasn't leaving. Not without having his say.

By the time he'd finished his drink, he realized the dinner had already started. Feeling calmer, he headed for the banquet room, which he'd mapped out earlier. When he got there, he immediately scanned the room, spying her at the correctly numbered table…the one where he'd arranged to be seated, too.

Not only had she come, she'd put on her female armor, obviously preparing herself to face him tonight.

She looked absolutely beautiful, almost as perfect now as she had when flashing him from beneath that robe. Not that she hadn't been practically perfect in his eyes when they'd bumped into each other this afternoon, of course. Nothing could hide the natural beauty of Lauren's heart-shaped face, the jewel-blue hue of her eyes or the thickness of her golden-brown hair, now hanging around her shoulders in thick waves. But unlike earlier, when she'd appeared frazzled and weary, she was absolutely put together now, wearing tasteful makeup, not a hair out of place, dressed in a blue cocktail dress that clung to her perfectly.

He'd bet she was wearing heels. Lauren wasn't short. In fact, she was of average height. But she'd always worn high-heeled shoes when she needed to build up her self-confidence.

He leaned his head to the side and swept his gaze downward, noting the long, shapely, bare legs. And her feet.

*Four inches. At least.* Spike-heeled power shoes that were supposed to make her feel tall and in control but just made her look sexy as hell.

He smiled as he wove his way toward her table. A few people recognized him and said hello, others merely raised curious brows, but he didn't pause. No way was he giving Lauren a chance to spot him and leave. She couldn't very well get up and march out the second he sat down, right?

He sat down. "Hello, everyone."

She stood up. "Goodbye, everyone."

Damn. She startled a laugh right out of him. But knowing better than to try to reason with her, he simply muttered, "Chicken."

She glared. "I'm not a chicken."

"What do you call running away?"

"Self-preservation."

"You don't have to protect yourself. I'm not trying to hurt you."

"Why not? It's what you do best."

"Ouch," somebody muttered.

They both looked around the table at the other half-dozen people, all of whom were watching them.

"Sit down, sweetie. Don't let him spoil your night," said the woman sitting on the other side of Lauren. Seth recognized her as Lauren's best friend.

"Hello, Maggie. Nice to see you."

The pretty blonde grunted. "I thought you were in prison."

"Sorry to disappoint you."

"Oh, you're good at disappointing people."

Another ouch. Lauren had an army of defenders, it appeared.

"It's all right, Maggie," said Lauren, slowly sinking back onto her chair. "He doesn't bother me."

"Certainly not intentionally," he insisted.

She rolled her eyes.

A guy Seth recognized from his senior English class offered him the first genuine smile he'd seen since he'd entered the room. "Nice to see you, Crowder."

"You, too, Josh."

"How's life? Where are you living these days?"

"West Coast."

Beside him, he saw Lauren yawn, as if she were completely uninterested. He didn't believe that, though. Tension rolled off her. Ambivalence usually didn't cause stiff shoulders, clenched fists and a defiantly uptilted chin.

"What do you do?" the other man asked.

"Actually, I'm a sports agent."

"Get out," the other man said, immediately intrigued as anyone with testosterone always was when they found out what he did for a living. If he mentioned the names of some of his clients, Josh would probably fall over.

Waving a hand to gloss over what was, if he did say so himself, a pretty cool job, he said, "I couldn't make it into the pros myself. Next best thing, I guess."

"We always thought you would," Josh replied, earnest and loyal as always. He smiled cautiously, casting an apologetic look at Lauren before adding, "I sometimes wondered if that's where you went—if you got drafted into the bigs and they wanted you in training right away."

"If only," Seth said. Then, aware he had Lauren's full attention—and also aware this might be the only time he had that attention, since she would be looking out for him now, knowing he'd manipulated himself into the seat beside her— he went ahead and came out with the truth.

"Nothing nearly as great as the NFL," he explained. "The real story is…"

Lauren shifted in her seat, leaning perhaps a hairsbreadth closer, as if she wanted to hear in spite of herself.

And he wasn't about to disappoint her with anything except the whole, utter truth.

"I disappeared because my crooked parents had to get out of the country fast, so they dragged me and my sister to somewhere without an extradition treaty."

LAUREN HADN'T WANTED to listen to Seth. Well, she'd wanted to listen, she just hadn't wanted to *hear* any of his excuses. It wasn't that she was scared, despite what he might think about the way she'd been avoiding him. The truth was, she'd always assumed there were no excuses worth hearing.

But the one that had come out of Seth's kissable mouth stopped her heart from beating for a few seconds. She couldn't breathe, could barely remain sitting upright. Because of all the things she'd imagined—good and bad—this definitely wasn't one of them.

"Holy shit, man, seriously?" asked Josh, taking the words right out of Lauren's mouth.

Seth reached for his water glass and lifted it. Lauren noticed the way the water sloshed on the top, and realized Seth's hand was shaking. He might be projecting a smooth, everything's-all-right attitude, but deep down, Seth was a mess. This confession, made so baldly in front of all these people, had cost him dearly. There was only one reason she could think of for him to throw it out there so publicly: because she wouldn't allow him to say it to her privately.

A hint of shame stabbed her. She cleared her throat. "You don't have to do this."

He shrugged. "Everybody's whispering about it, anyway. Might as well let the truth mingle in with all the stories."

"You're not kidding, are you?" Maggie asked, the sneer gone, her pretty green eyes big and round.

"I wish I were."

"How come we never heard about it?" Josh asked.

"I don't think there was a lot of news coverage until later, when the feds caught up with them."

One question answered. His parents were, apparently, no longer in hiding. Guess that nonextraditing country hadn't been such a safe haven after all.

"By then, you'd all graduated and I was old news. I don't think my name was ever in the papers, either."

Even if it had been, Lauren wouldn't have seen it. She'd left Chicago a few weeks after graduation, once she'd realized Seth really wasn't coming back. And she'd never—despite being tempted on a few occasions—gone looking for news of him on the internet.

"How…what…wow, they dragged you out of the country?" asked Maggie.

"Yeah. I had gone home the night before and stayed there so I could borrow my Dad's car to drive to the prom."

Lauren nodded slowly, remembering. He'd talked about that—insisting he wanted to take her in style in his dad's Porsche.

"I woke up that morning preparing to go pick up my tux and a corsage for Lauren. Then I came downstairs to find my father shoving cash in a briefcase and my mother scooping up the silver from the dining room. They told me there was an emergency, they were in danger and we were moving. Immediately."

The conversation in the banquet room had quieted significantly, and Lauren realized everybody within earshot had shut up to hear the juicy details firsthand.

"I didn't find out the truth until we were on a plane somewhere over Central America," Seth continued. "Dear old Dad apparently went to the Bernie Madoff school of financial management, though on a much smaller scale. My mom helped him, and they knew they were about to be arrested."

He said it easily, but she heard the heartbreak there, and honestly couldn't imagine it. She had never met Seth's parents, but she knew they had never come to a single school event. She had the feeling he and his sister were treated as out-of-sight, out-of-mind tax deductions. Still, she couldn't imagine having the blinders torn off your eyes like that, finding out your wealthy, well-respected parents were wanted criminals.

As if he knew the question everybody wanted to ask, he continued. "I'm sure you're wondering why I went. I was eighteen, and I could have thrown a fit and refused to go with them. But to be honest, I was kinda shell-shocked. Remember, I didn't know the whole story at first—I was imagining a hit being put out on my dad by the mob or something. Not the FBI."

Of course, what eighteen-year-old kid after being told by his parents that they were in danger wouldn't think something dire like that? It was certainly more logical than the wanted-by-the-authorities explanation.

"Mainly, I was worried about Em, who *wasn't* eighteen and had no choice. When she was a baby, my parents wouldn't have remembered to feed her if it was the maid's day off."

He had always been close and protective of his sister, who had been in seventh grade at the time. At just twelve or thirteen, her whole world had been shaken apart, as Seth's had been.

He had been speaking to everyone, but he suddenly turned his attention to Lauren. "I had time to make one phone call. I was told exactly what to say, and my father was standing there the whole time to make sure I didn't say anything else. I'm so sorry I stood you up that night, Lauren."

She didn't respond. She'd spent so many years being angry at him. To say she was confused would be an understatement. She had more questions, of course, but wasn't sure she had the right to ask them. He was, after all, telling this story to everyone, not just to her. If he wanted anybody to know more, he'd say it.

He didn't, falling silent while buzzing conversations resumed at their own table and at those near enough to have overheard. This would be the talk of the reunion.

"Seth, I don't know what to say," she finally replied.

More than that, she didn't know what to feel. She'd spent so many years resenting him for breaking her heart, imagining a million things, but nothing close to the truth. Now, though, she wasn't sure what to call the emotions racing through her, making her stomach churn, her fists clench, her eyes sting.

Indignation, of course—on his behalf, and his sister's.

Anger at his parents. A huge amount of curiosity about what else had happened. How had Seth ended up back in the U.S.? And when?

Yeah. Lots of questions. But none she wanted to ask in front of any of these people. She wasn't sure he'd want to answer them, even in private, but she had to at least try. So, taking a deep breath and telling herself she owed him the chance to clear the air, and owed herself the chance to learn the truth and forgive him, she pushed back from the table.

Rising to her feet, she glanced at Seth, seeing the flash of disappointment on his face and hearing his sigh. Did he think she was leaving? Walking out without a word? Was he so used to rejection and revulsion when other people heard about his family that he automatically expected it?

Her heart—frozen and hardened against him such a long time ago—thawed the tiniest bit. They weren't kids anymore, and far too much time had gone by for anything to happen between them. Not to mention the geography issue. But that didn't mean she couldn't give Seth the atonement he seemed to need.

"Come on," she told him, seeing the way his head jerked in surprise. "Let's get out of here and go talk."

## 3

SHE DIDN'T HAVE TO ASK him twice. Seth wasn't about to stick around with these wide-eyed people who were dying to put their heads together in titillation over his confession: that the golden-boy king of the prom was the son of a couple of crooks. He'd come here for one reason—Lauren. Her finally agreeing to talk to him made the trip from California worthwhile.

He got up, nodded to the others at the table and took Lauren's arm. She fell into step beside him, their strides matching, as if she was just as eager to escape as he was. Her long leg brushed against his trousers and her bare shoulder was inches from his own, their hands touching as they both reached for the door handle.

The excitement was catching; it was as if they'd both realized they were going to share a moment ten years in the making. Finally, they could clear the air, answer the questions, ask for and offer forgiveness.

His heart was pounding. Seth had never been more aware of a woman, never so desperate to breathe deeper to catch her scent, to touch her to make sure she was real and here, ready to give him a chance to explain. Everything about her called to a nearly forgotten part of him, that deep, secret place where he'd once been young and crazy in love.

Not to mention in lust.

He'd wanted Lauren desperately the entire time they'd dated, but he'd been the "good" boyfriend and made do with heavy petting and deep, hungry make-out sessions that usually left him blue-balled and needing to visit his own hand. Knowing they were supposed to consummate their relationship on prom night had been like racing for the end of the rainbow to get the pot of gold.

Instead, he'd spent that night running away from everything he knew with his cold, selfish parents, already mourning what he had lost…and what he'd never had.

He hadn't come here to have sex with Lauren. But he wasn't a liar. If the opportunity presented itself, he'd take it and never look back. Because he thought it might kill him if he lived his entire life without ever knowing what it would be like to make love to her.

He was about to ask where she wanted to go when she said, "I need a drink. Let's find the nearest bar."

"Good plan," he said with a nod.

He didn't steer her toward the saloon, which had been heating up with a raucous crowd when he'd left a short time ago. Nor was he interested in the '50s Sock Hop Hall, the '70s Disco, or the '80s Techno Club. The piano bar sounded like the best place for them to sit in a shadowy corner undisturbed.

Fortunately, most of the reunions being held at Celebrations this weekend had similar opening dinners tonight. So while the banquet rooms were filled to the brim, the small piano lounge was almost completely empty.

She spied the same back corner table he did, and strode toward it. A waitress met them there and Lauren said, "Vodka martini. Dirty. And make it a double."

Hiding his smile, Seth murmured, "I'll have the same."

He sat across from her, letting his eyes adjust to the low lighting, liking the way the amber table light cast shadows on her gold-streaked hair. It wasn't quite as long as it had been in high school, but was still thick and beautiful. He remembered burying his hands in it when they kissed. Many times.

"So. Dragged to a foreign country by your fleeing-the-law parents," she finally said, holding his steady gaze. "I guess that qualifies as a decent excuse for not coming to prom."

A tiny smile tugged at his mouth. "Have I mentioned our flight was so turbulent, I got sick in my mom's purse?"

"On the silver?"

"They wouldn't let her carry it on. But I ruined her designer wallet."

"Was it really airsickness?" she asked, seeing through the humor and getting right to the point.

He shook his head. "No. It wasn't."

He'd been physically ill all right…sick about what his parents had done, that he'd let them drag him along, about what would happen to Emily. The minute he'd found out the truth, he'd started to argue, demanding to be returned home. His pleas had fallen on deaf ears. And when he truly accepted the fact that his father—who he'd assumed was inattentive because he was busy making millions of dollars for other people—had been stealing those dollars, he'd literally thrown up.

He had to be honest with himself. If he'd been able to call Lauren sooner, he might not have done it. He'd been pretty ashamed for the first few months of his unwanted exile.

As if she knew that, she reached across the table and gently squeezed his hand. It was meant to be comforting, quick, friendly. But Seth found himself gripping her fingers, holding tight. He was flooded with memories of innocent days when holding Lauren's hand had felt like the most momentous part of his day.

Her fingers were still soft, fragile, slender. He wanted

them touching him, twining in his hair, pulling him close for a warm, sultry kiss.

Their stares met and locked for a long second. Then, knowing they still had talking to do, he released her.

The silence continued as the waitress returned with their drinks. Lauren took a sip of hers, then lowered the glass back onto the table and ran the tip of her finger across its wet rim.

"So then what happened?" she finally asked.

He didn't really want to get into the whole story, but he'd promised her—and himself—that he wouldn't hold anything back if she gave him the chance to speak. So he told her, trying not to dwell on the dark details or let his voice reveal the still-tangled emotions he carried with him and probably always would.

When he was finished, she peppered him with questions. "Did you even know which country you were in?"

"Not at first."

"And you didn't have any money?"

"Not a cent. Or my passport. They took it."

"There was no phone, no computer at the house they rented?"

"No computer. They had a satellite phone they kept under lock and key in a safe in their bedroom." Knowing the other questions she had to be wondering about, he added, "The servants all spoke Spanish, and I didn't. Plus the estate they rented was in the middle of nowhere. The times we went into the nearest town, my parents never let us out of their sight. Em and I pretty much just had each other."

She bit her lip and blinked quickly, as if trying to hide any telltale moisture in her eyes. "How did you get away?" she asked, her voice soft, a whisper.

"I cracked the safe," he admitted, smiling at the memory.

"Seriously?"

"It was pretty old. I worked on it for months. Finally, I

opened it, got a hold of the phone and called my grandfather in California."

"Did he come for you?"

"He waited long enough to get a visa, then hopped on a plane to South America," he replied, wondering if she could hear the relief and gratitude he still felt, all these years later. His grandfather had been the best man he'd ever known, had been everything Seth's own father wasn't. Honest, loving, honorable, he'd been a straight-arrow high school football coach who'd never understood the woman his daughter had become when she'd married Seth's rich father. Seth had known his Gramps would know what to do. And he had.

"How…"

"I was able to tell him the country and the name of the nearest town. He showed up a week after my call for help. He told my parents he'd already called the FBI and turned them in. Demanding our passports, he packed up me and Em and flew us back stateside."

"When was that?"

"October '02. Almost five months after we left Chicago. He took us back to live with him in L.A." Seth reached for his own drink, sipping and letting the icy liquid cool off the heat of the memories. "That was the week I called you at your parents' house." Not sure what answer he wanted, he asked, "I guess you didn't get the message?"

"I got it."

Oh. She'd chosen not to call him back. A part of him had been hoping she'd say her parents had never told her he'd been trying to find her. "I understand. I guess you'd moved on and didn't want to hear any excuses."

"True, though I probably would have listened to them at that point. I didn't get quite as hard and angry until a few years had gone by without any further word."

Unable to help it, he asked, "So why didn't you call me back?"

Her eyes widened in shock. "Call you… What do you mean?"

"I gave your father my number and asked him to have you call me in California. I even offered to fly to Chicago to explain and to apologize to you and your family in person."

She lifted a hand to her face, rubbing her eyes, sighing audibly. "I didn't get that part of the message." Shaking her head, she said, "My mother was the one who told me you'd called to apologize, but nothing else. I guess my father only told her what he wanted either of us to hear, because I know she wouldn't have kept that from me."

Seth wasn't sure whether he felt better, or worse. Part of him was relieved she hadn't chosen to ignore him for the past decade. Another part hated that she'd been manipulated by her own father, as he had by his. Of course, hers had almost certainly been doing it for her own good. His…not so much.

"That's a lot of lost years due to other people's interference," he mumbled, talking as much to himself as to her.

"Maybe we needed them in order to grow up."

"Maybe." Then, getting to the point that had brought him here, he added, "So do you think you can forgive me for running out on you without a word?"

Lauren stared at him across the table. Her eyes were decidedly glassy now, and she was nibbling her bottom lip. The hand that continued to toy with the rim of her glass shook.

But her words were steady. Absolutely certain.

"I can. And I do, Seth. You're forgiven."

He nodded slowly and replied, "Thank you."

LAUREN HADN'T TOTALLY understood how much her acceptance of Seth's apology meant to him until she saw the way he sagged back in his chair in relief. He looked like a criminal who'd been forgiven by his victim.

In truth, he'd been the victim…of unscrupulous parents, of time, of distance, of her resentment and her father's overprotectiveness. She wanted to cry for him, and for Emily. They hadn't even talked about what had happened later. Were his parents in prison? Still on the run? How had he ended up working as a sports agent and how had Emily ended up back here in Illinois?

There were a lot of questions still to be answered. But right now, she didn't want to ask them. She just wanted to sit here, enjoying the soft music and his company, letting herself believe, for the first time in ten years, that he really had, at one time, cared about her. She wasn't going to call it love— eighteen-year-old guys didn't really understand that concept as far as she was concerned. But he'd cared. And that mattered to her. A lot.

"So how's *your* life been?" he finally asked with a wry chuckle, breaking the silence.

She laughed with him. "Not bad. I live in Georgia now."

His jaw dropped. "Seriously? I can't picture you as a slow-talking, languid Southern belle."

A hint of an accent had crept into his remark, and she responded in kind. "Why, suh, you wound me. Ah'm a genteel Georgia peach."

His laughter turned into a snort. "You might have a Georgia zip code, but your blood's all Chicago speed and energy."

Maybe. Probably. She definitely wasn't happy with her job, and hadn't been since her much-loved boss, Mimi, had left the grocery store chain her family owned. Frankly, laying out ads for canned green beans and dog food hadn't been what she'd had in mind when she'd gotten her marketing degree.

Seth's open smile and easy charm made him so easy to talk to that she found herself telling him all about it. He soon had her spilling her guts about her life, everywhere she'd been in the past ten years, every address, job…and relationship.

Those hadn't been hard to talk about—they'd been few and far between. But the conversation had opened the door, and since turnabout was fair play, she eventually asked, "What about you? No Mrs. Crowder back in L.A., I take it?"

He almost choked on his drink. Setting it down, he leaned over the table and said, "You really think I'd have tracked you down and tried so desperately to make things right with you if I had a wife?"

Not wanting to read too much into his words, which made it sound as though he'd come here for more than an apology, she kept her tone light. "It's possible. Maybe you're doing some kind of twelve-step program and making amends is part of it."

He gestured toward his empty martini glass. "If so, I'm doing a pretty shitty job with the rest of the program."

"True."

"I came here because I wanted the chance to explain, to make sure you understood. I've been angry at my parents for a lot of reasons for a lot of years."

"I don't blame you."

He went on as if she hadn't spoken. "But close to the top of the list is that they cost me you." His jaw clenched and his hand tightened on his glass. His voice low, he added, "They cost me the night we were supposed to share after the prom."

Lauren's heart skipped a beat. She'd been letting down her guard, enjoying being with him, remembering how wonderful Seth had been to talk to. She'd almost forgotten the sexual tension that swam between them when they were together. Now she was reminded of it. His lips parted as he breathed across them, his eyes narrowed as he swept a thorough stare over her hair, her face, her throat, her chest. Oh, yeah, there was lots of tension.

He looked away. "Sorry."

He wanted her. Still. There was no denying it. Maybe he had come here for forgiveness, but he'd also come here because of the sex they'd never had.

Was there anything men wanted more than the one who got away? She didn't think so. Funny, though, she wasn't offended by it. In fact, she had to take a moment to pull her thoughts back in order, and decide *what* she was feeling. She'd been telling herself, ever since she'd heard his voice at the registration desk, that Seth being here was a bad thing. Feeling the electricity zapping between them during that oh-so-brief kiss when she'd caught him outside her room had reinforced that idea.

Now, though, she couldn't decide if things had gotten better or worse. She had forgiven him, she did understand and she was still incredibly attracted to him. As he, apparently, was to her.

Could she have him, though? They barely knew each other anymore, with a decade's worth of resentment and misery between them. They lived on opposite sides of the country for heaven's sake!

Still, he wasn't talking about a relationship, about love. He was talking about sex. About attraction, curiosity, regret and the need to finally have something they'd both been denied.

She wouldn't have trusted declarations of love, not after all this time. But sexual desire? That she could trust. That she could rely on. That she could even indulge.

"It meant that much to you?"

"Are you serious?"

She nodded slowly.

Seth leaned closer over the table, until the tips of his fingers brushed hers, and she could feel the warmth of his exhalations against her cheek.

"It meant *everything* to me, Lauren."

She had to shift in her seat, her entire body going on alert at the tone in his voice. He was so sure, so certain, so unmistakable about his desire for her.

"I'd had sex before, you knew that."

Yes, she'd known. And she honestly had wondered why he was being patient, waiting for her, the innocent virgin.

"But it was like I was starting over again with you. Getting the chance to do it the right way, for the right reasons, with the right person."

"Yeah, tell me about it. I ended up with the *wrong* person because I was so angry at you."

He swiped a frustrated hand through his thick hair. "One more thing to add to my list of crimes."

She reached out and grabbed his other hand, not wanting him to take on that burden of guilt, as well. "It's okay. Women survive bad sex."

"So do guys."

"Had your fair share, huh?"

He nodded. "I never got past the wondering. I compared every woman I got involved with to the possibility of what it would have been like with you."

She understood. Because she'd done the same thing for ten long years.

Suddenly she realized those years didn't matter. What had happened in the past didn't matter. What would happen tomorrow didn't matter.

There was only tonight. They had it. They deserved it.

And she wanted it.

"I think it's time we found out, don't you?" she asked, hearing the invitation in her own lowered, sultry voice.

"What are you—"

She cut him off, knowing what she wanted and not wanting to dance around it anymore. "I'm saying, Seth, that I want the night we never had. Now."

He didn't respond, didn't accept her invitation—or, probably more accurately, her challenge. Because whether she'd meant it that way or not, her tone had dared him to take her up on her offer.

She held her breath, waiting to see if he would. Then, without saying anything, he pushed his chair back, threw a wad of cash on the table and took her arm.

*Guess that's a yes.*

"I would say your room or mine, but frankly, I'm not sure I'm even going to make it past the elevator," he admitted.

Her legs shook and every feminine part of her softened with need at the sound of desperation in his voice. Because it was matched by her own. "The first private spot will be fine."

As luck would have it, however, there was no private spot between them and the elevator. In fact, to Lauren's extreme consternation, as soon as they left the lounge, they ran into several people from their class, who had left the dinner and were now heading out to sample the various entertainments Celebrations had to offer.

Everyone begged her and Seth to join them, but Lauren had a much different celebration in mind. The reunion she was looking forward to would happen in a bed—his or hers, it didn't matter which—and would involve sultry pleasure and a long night filled with passion.

Or so she hoped.

*God, what if it's no good? What if he's no good?*

Scratch that. He'd be good. She had no doubt of it.

But what if he thought she was no good?

Suddenly feeling doubts, she let her feet drag as their former class president, Roseanne something, who had also been one of Seth's old flames, stepped right into their path. The woman hadn't changed much—still rich, still beautiful, apparently still a raging bitch.

"Oh, come on, Seth, you have to come with us. You owe

me a dance. After all, we never got to finish dancing at the spring formal in our junior year, remember?" She cast Lauren a catty look. "We left early."

"I remember *you* leaving early," Lauren said, meowing back as good as she got. "Weren't you the one who got so drunk, you passed out and didn't even realize a freshman drove you home?"

Beside her, Seth chuckled and whispered, "That was *Sixteen Candles.*"

"Shut up," she hissed back, enjoying watching Roseanne sputter.

"That's not funny!"

"Sure it is," Lauren replied. "Come on, Roseanne, you were totally wasted. And Seth wasn't even your date that year. He went with, hmm, who was it?"

"Sharon Stillwater," he said, unabashed, obviously enjoying himself.

"You were such a dog," Lauren couldn't help replying.

"Only until you finally gave me the time of day."

His smile tender, he slipped an arm around her waist, visibly saying to everyone else what hadn't yet been put into words: the prom king had finally claimed his queen. At least for tonight.

Even Roseanne shut her mouth as Seth led Lauren toward their tower, heading for the elevators. Lauren imagined there would be a lot of gossip flying around this place tonight. Tomorrow's carnival and formal dance would probably turn into interrogation sessions, and her friend Maggie would probably be lead inquisitor.

But she'd worry about that tomorrow. Tonight, she didn't have a care in the world. She was going to live, to take what she had wanted for such a long time, and enjoy the hell out of it.

As they waited for the elevators, Seth murmured, "I really was a bit of a player, wasn't I?"

"Not really. Just a typical high school superstar."

"Why'd you ever agree to go out with me?" he asked, looking truly curious. "I must have asked you a dozen times before you finally said yes in our senior year."

She didn't have to think about it. The memory was emblazoned in her mind. "I saw you with Em, comforting her."

He raised a curious brow.

"It was about a week after 9/11, when classes started again."

He swallowed visibly, the way everyone probably did when thinking about those awful days.

"I was walking to the bus stop, and passed you sitting on a bench, holding her hands. She looked like she'd been crying, and you were reassuring her that she would be all right, that you wouldn't let anything happen to her."

He nodded. "She had bad dreams for weeks. My parents were in New York when it happened. It took them two days to think about their children, to call and tell us they weren't dead."

She remembered him telling her that, later. Remembered the quiver in his voice, the moisture in his eyes.

But not as well as she remembered that September afternoon, passing by them as they sat on the bench, witnessing Seth's tender care of his sister. That was the moment she'd realized there was so much more to him than the rest of the world ever gave him credit for. It was also probably the moment she started to fall in love with him.

She turned toward him, rose on tiptoe and brushed her lips across his jaw. His sandpapery skin was rough against her mouth, but she loved the roughness, the raw masculine power of him and couldn't wait to experience it on other parts of her body.

"I saw the real you that day," she whispered. "I decided he was somebody I wanted to know better."

And soon, she was going to know him as thoroughly and completely as a woman could ever know a man.

It was their long-promised night. At last.

# 4

Seth managed to keep his hands to himself, at least until they were inside the elevator. Alone. The minute the doors swished shut, however, all bets were off.

There was a camera above them. He didn't give a damn.

"Come here," he ordered, grabbing her waist and pulling her close.

Lauren didn't resist. Melting against him, she lifted her arms around his neck. Their mouths came together in a fast, hard kiss, their tongues plunging in a frenzied mating that had been building for ten years.

She tasted like heaven. Like Lauren. Familiar and sweet and sultry and so impossibly good.

He'd kissed other women over the years, but none had felt as right, as perfectly made for him. He hadn't imagined it. All the times he'd wondered if there really was such a thing as a soul mate, the one right person for everyone, he'd remembered how it had felt to kiss her. But he'd also wondered if his memories were lying to him.

They weren't. She was perfect...for him, anyway.

He kissed her hard and deep, as if to remind them both of that, to drive thoughts of any other man out of her head for good, and to imprint her on his own, lest he ever have doubts again.

Lauren writhed against him, her soft body curving into all his angles, asking and answering all at the same time. They shared breaths and their heartbeats pounded in unison. The silence was broken only by their sighs, and by the ding of the elevator as it went up, up, up, taking them toward what he was sure must be heaven on earth.

But not fast enough. He needed more. Needed to taste her, touch her. "God, Lauren, I've wanted you forever," he said as he moved his mouth to her neck.

She twined her fingers in his hair and held him tight, as if unwilling to let him go. "Ditto."

Their mouths came together again, slower this time. He dropped his hands to her hips, pulling her more firmly against his groin, and heard her groan as she felt how hard and ready he was for her.

"Ahem."

They'd been so lost in the kiss, they hadn't even noticed that the elevator had stopped and someone had boarded it. Seth forced himself to let her go. Glancing over, he saw an older couple eyeing them speculatively. The man was grinning, the woman—mid-forties and very attractive—was studying the number panel on the side of the elevator. But Seth noticed the way a flush of color rose in her face, and how her companion slipped an arm around her waist, giving her bottom a familiar pat.

Once the other couple got off a few floors later, he heard Lauren begin to laugh.

"I think if we hadn't been here, *they'd* have been the ones shocking the security camera guys. Something about this place makes everyone want to…celebrate."

That was true. He'd seen cozy couples in the lounges, and sitting on plush couches in the lobby. The resort might have been made for group reunions, but it seemed to also invite gatherings of a more intimate sort.

"Maybe it's because a reunion, by definition, brings you back to your younger years, when you were freer, more willing to take risks." He nuzzled her neck. "And indulge in pleasures. Take what you most want."

She gazed up at him, licking her reddened lips. "Makes sense to me."

They at last arrived on their floor. Seth grabbed her hand and practically dragged her after him. Her room was closer, but he didn't want to wait long enough for her to dig the key out of her purse. His was in his pocket, and then, a second later, in his hand.

"You *had* to have set this up. There must be a thousand rooms in this place," she said, laughter on her lips as he led her to a door not far from her own.

"Yep."

"Remind me to thank Em when I see her."

Lauren meant that from the bottom of her heart. She didn't know what had brought Seth's sister back to Chicago or how she'd ended up working at this resort. She was just thankful Emily had been able to let Seth know Lauren would be here. She didn't want to think about the possibility that she might have gone through the rest of her life not knowing the truth.

Or not having this night.

The moment they walked into Seth's room, laid out much the same as hers, they melted into each other's arms again. Their kisses were still hungry, still demanding, but also slower. They had all night. She wanted to enjoy every minute of it.

"Touch me, please," she whispered.

He did, stroking her face, her throat, her shoulders. She sighed as he reached around to unzip her dress, drawing the tab down ever so slowly. His fingertips brushed against her spine, making her shiver. All that heat against her cool skin.

When the dress was completely unfastened, he drew it off her shoulders. Lauren's heart raced as the soft fabric fell in a puddle at her feet and Seth stepped back to look at her.

"You're even more beautiful than I remembered." His voice shook with honesty and need.

She smiled, lifted an arm and pushed her hair back, knowing her breasts were thrust out in invitation.

He accepted.

Pulling her to him, Seth bent to nuzzle the top curves of her breasts, breathing through the satiny fabric of her bra. Her nipples were already pebbled with desire, and when his mouth closed over one, she felt her legs weaken.

He didn't let her fall, of course. Instead, he reached down and swooped her up into his arms, still kissing her chest. Striding over to the king-size bed, he gently lowered her onto the mattress, following her down.

Lauren still wore her black bra and panties, and her wickedly spike-heeled shoes. But Seth was even more overdressed.

"Those. Off," she ordered, pointing to his clothes.

"Yes, ma'am."

He stood beside the bed and shrugged out of his suit jacket. Beneath, his perfectly tailored dress shirt emphasized the broadness of his shoulders, the bulging muscles in his upper arms. He said he worked as a sports agent, but Seth was obviously still very active himself.

She licked her lips. Coveting. Hungry.

"You're so big," she whispered as he unbuttoned the shirt, revealing the muscled chest, the rippling stomach.

As she recalled, he was big everywhere.

No, they'd never had intercourse, but they'd definitely done…other things. Seth wasn't the only one who'd enjoyed giving oral sex. Remembering his taste, his essence, she ached to experience him that way again. Sitting up, she scooted to the edge of the bed, parting her legs so he could step between them. She unfastened his belt, pulled it free, then reached for his pants button. Pressing her mouth to the perfect male abdomen, she dipped her tongue into his belly button, then tasted her way down as she drew the zipper lower.

He wore tight boxer briefs, which strained to contain the huge ridge of aroused male. She pressed her tongue to a damp spot at the top of the fabric, and was pleased to feel him shudder in response.

"You know I love that, but I'm not going to settle for it this time," he told her, his voice shaking.

"Just a taste," she demanded.

Not waiting for permission, she pulled the briefs down, revealing his rigid cock to her covetous eyes. She dipped her head, flicked her tongue over the silky-smooth tip, holding his hips when he jerked.

His hands moved to her head, and he gently twined his fingers in her hair. Lauren took that as his approval of what she was doing…not that she had intended to wait for it.

Easing the briefs down, she moved her mouth lower. Taking him inch by inch, wetting him with her tongue, she sucked him the way she knew he loved to be sucked. He didn't move, didn't pull her or try to control what she was doing. He just took the pleasure she offered.

Loving the fullness in her mouth—the taste, the smell, the brush of the spiky curls on his groin against her face, she continued pleasuring him. Knowing what else he liked, she slid her hand down, squeezing the base of his cock, then cupping the vulnerable sacs beneath.

"Enough," he snapped, pulling back. He almost stumbled on his pants, still twisted around his legs. His hand shaking, he pointed a finger at her. "I've been waiting ten years for this, I'm not going to let you have me ready to shoot off like a rocket the second I finally get inside your beautiful body."

She did feel beautiful, and desired. Seth was a picture of masculine need as he stared at her from a few feet away.

"We have all night," she reminded him.

"And I plan to spend at least several hours of it buried inside you."

Every inch of her tingled in excitement. Because it wasn't a threat…it was a promise.

Never taking his eyes off her, Seth tore off the rest of his clothes, then returned to the bed. "Your turn. Those. Off," he said, pointing to her bra and panties. Then, with a definite eyebrow wag, he added, "But feel free to leave the shoes."

She grinned. "Aye-aye, sir."

Smoothing her palms over her midriff, knowing he watched the way her hands moved over her body, she reached up and toyed with her bra. Her fingertips traced her hard nipples, plucking them, then tugging the fabric down to expose them to his gaze.

Seth swallowed visibly, but made no move toward her.

He liked watching her touch herself. She remembered that, too.

Pulling one strap down and exposing a breast, she continued to stroke herself, tweaking her nipple, imagining it was Seth's hand, Seth's mouth. As the pleasure built, her hips arched up, undulating as her body sought a much-needed rhythm.

Keeping one hand at her breast, she moved the other one down, knowing she was performing for him. She'd never felt this free with any other man, never wanted to pleasure herself while he watched. But something made her slide her fingertips below the elastic edge of her skimpy panties and tangle them in the soft nest of curls between her thighs.

"Let me see," he ordered with a groan.

She nudged the panties down, loving the way his lids half closed over his eyes, the stare sultry, hot as he saw her rub her clit.

"Let me give you a hand," he offered.

"Thanks ever so much," she replied with a wicked smile as he tugged her panties down, and all the way off. He had to work them over the shoes, but she knew he'd want the shoes to stay on for as long as possible.

Once her panties were gone, Seth watched her a moment more. Then his control broke. With a groan, he swept her hand out of the way and bent over her. He gave her no warning, replacing her fingertips with his tongue, licking her fast and deep.

She cried out and nearly came off the bed.

"Shh," he said, his mouth buried in her sex. "Let me."

Let him? She might kill him if he stopped.

Oh, he definitely didn't stop. He plunged his tongue deep, then swirled it over her throbbing clitoris. Within moments, she felt an orgasm breaking over her like violent waves crashing on a beach during a storm. She shook all over with it.

Seth moved up, tasting his way up her body, kissing her from groin to chest. There he stopped, taking a pleasurable detour over her breasts and nipples. When he sucked one, hard, while tweaking the other, the nearly gone orgasm reared up again, sending another blast of pleasure rocketing through her.

"God, how do you *do* that?" she gasped.

No one else had ever made her respond like this.

"We're just getting started," he reminded her before moving his mouth to hers and kissing her deeply. Their tongues met, the kiss flavored by the musky essence of both their bodies, which made it hotter, more wanton.

"I need you inside me, Seth," she begged.

He paused, glancing toward the floor where his clothes lay in a heap. "I should get…"

"I'm on the Pill. And I've always been…careful."

He nodded, understanding what she meant. She'd never had condomless sex with anyone. But she wanted it now, wanted their first time to be completely natural, wanted his skin against hers.

"So am I," he said. "I don't sleep around."

"Then love me, Seth," she whispered.

He nodded, his eyes locked on hers as he moved between her parted thighs. She wrapped her legs around him, pulling him closer, urging him on, until she felt the heat of his erection nudging at her sex.

Ten years of waiting had made her impatient. And while Seth tried to move slowly, carefully, as if wanting to be sure he wouldn't hurt her, she wasn't having it.

"Take me now," she demanded, thrusting up to meet him.

He groaned and gave in to her plea, jerking his hips, burying himself in her so deeply she thought she'd split in half.

Lauren screamed. Not with pain. Because nothing had ever felt so good. He was inside her, part of her, filling her up in a way only he could do.

"Okay?" he asked.

"So okay."

She wrapped her arms around his neck, drawing him down for a kiss, wanting every inch of their bodies to touch. They stayed still, joined, acknowledging the moment, giving it the attention it deserved.

"It's been a long wait," he whispered.

"But a worthwhile one?"

"Oh, God, yes," he said, his voice firm and certain.

At last they began to move, rocking together in perfect harmony. He gave and she took, then she gave right back.

It went on. And on. She lost track of time and reality, focused only on his deep strokes inside her, the smell of him, the weight of him on top of her. Eventually, they rolled over, so Lauren could ride him, look down at his incredibly handsome face and amazing body.

She came again. Once, maybe twice. And still he showed no sign of being near completion.

He hadn't been kidding about making love to her for hours. Which was fine with her. This night had been ten years in the making…. She was in no hurry for it to end.

Especially because she had absolutely no idea what tomorrow would bring.

ALTHOUGH SETH HAD WANTED her to stay in bed with him and order room service Saturday morning, Lauren had promised Maggie she would meet her for breakfast. Considering she'd come here because her friend needed her, she couldn't blow her off. So, telling Seth she'd meet him at the carnival later, she headed to her room to shower and change, then went down to one of the many restaurants to meet her friend.

Her mood was good—great, in fact. She'd never had a better night in her life, and it obviously showed. Maggie took one look at her and demanded details. Lauren told her as much as was ladylike…and then a bit more, grinning all the while. Maggie, who was pretty anti-men/anti-romance right now, cheered her on, declaring Lauren had every right to have meaningless sex with her high school dreamboat.

Meaningless. That word echoed. As she devoured her breakfast, ravenous after her lack of dinner the previous night—followed by hours of wonderful exertion—the doubts crept in.

Yes, she'd had a wonderful night. But was Maggie right? Did it mean absolutely nothing? If so, how wise would it be to spend another day—and night—with Seth, knowing they'd be flying to other sides of the country, with no promises made or asked for, not even a suggestion that they might have more than this weekend?

Lauren wasn't the Goody Two-shoes she had been in high school. But she wasn't the one-night-stand type, either. Yet, the longer she talked to her friend, the more she felt like she'd just had one.

"If I were smart, I'd get out while the going's good," Lauren finally mumbled.

Maggie scowled. "Are you serious?"

"As a heart attack."

"That's crazy talk. Get as much good stuff as you can out of the man until tomorrow, then walk away knowing you've had great sex with a guy who's never going to break your heart again…because it's not his to break this time."

Ouch. Lauren only wished she could agree. She feared, however, that she couldn't. Seth had owned her heart once upon a time, and he had staked a claim on it again last night.

"You think that's all there is to it?" she asked.

"Of course. You got what you wanted, had a fantastic, amazing night together, and can have another fantastic one tonight. So do it, then go home and forget all about him."

Forget about him? Fat chance. "I don't know if I can."

Maggie rolled her eyes. "You're overanalyzing this. It's just sex, Lauren. Don't go thinking there are feelings involved."

No feelings? Ha. There had definitely been feelings in that bed last night.

"I mean, it's not like he said he loved you, right?" Lauren's expression obviously answered that question, because Maggie went right on. "Which is a damn good thing, because that would be crazy. Teenage boys don't fall in love, and don't continue to love the same person without laying eyes on them for ten years. He's a Hollywood sports agent for heaven's sake. He's probably had dozens of affairs."

She didn't want to think about him with anyone else. He'd

sounded so sincere last night when he told her he didn't sleep around.

"Believe me, if he had said he loved you, I'd be telling you to run the other way. Because you'd be getting played."

Maggie was right—ten years was more than a third of their lifetimes. So of course he couldn't love her. Or she him.

Right?

"As long as there are no pesky emotions on the table, and he's being totally honest about what he came for, I say take what you get, then go home and forget it."

"I don't know…."

It sounded so cold, not to mention risky. The wise thing would be for her to get in her rental car, drive back to Chicago, spend a nice afternoon and evening with her parents, then fly back to Georgia tomorrow. And never see Seth again.

That was the heart-wise thing to do, anyway. Not the body-wise one. Her body wanted to go right back to his room with a jar of this delicious maple syrup and lick it off every inch of his incredibly sexy skin.

"I mean, you're not still mad at him, right?" Maggie asked, obviously missing Lauren's true problem. Maybe because she was so bitter about love, given her ex-husband's cheating, she didn't even want to see it anymore.

"Definitely not."

After their conversation, and his explanation, she felt only tenderness toward the man—well, toward the teenage boy she'd known. She couldn't imagine what it had been like for him, finding out his parents were such unpleasant people, then getting dragged away from everyone and everything he knew. How desperate and lonely he must have been, trapped by his need to protect his sister, penniless and helpless in a foreign country. Honestly, she didn't know many eighteen year olds who could have handled it and not come out the other end a complete wreck.

Seth had come out of it a wonderful, funny, sexy, charming, successful man.

That was the problem. Because he *was* charming, friendly, funny and sexy. It would be *way* too easy to fall in love with him again. She'd felt those crazy, butterfly-in-the-stomach feelings toward him the minute she'd laid eyes on him again. Being in his arms during the most erotic night of her life had done a great job of splintering the wall she'd built around her heart. A wall she needed if she was going to survive having him walk out of her life again, as quickly as he'd walked back into it.

"Well, you'd better decide quick," Maggie said, glancing past Lauren toward the entrance to the restaurant. "Because here he comes."

She stiffened, then, trying to be casual about it, turned to glance over her shoulder. Seth was walking toward their table, sexier than a man had a right to be. His thick, dark hair was damp from his shower. Wearing a faded T-shirt and soft, washed-out jeans, he looked completely at ease. Not to mention satisfied.

"Sorry to interrupt your breakfast, but I was asked to find you both. They need volunteers to man some of the games at the carnival."

"Games? Yippie," said Maggie. "How about I man the 'pin the tail on the asshole ex-husband' booth?"

Seth grinned. "I think they have you down for the ring-toss."

"'Ring around the asshole ex-husband,' then. I can do that," she said as she rose.

Seth then looked at Lauren. "So, what do you say? Ready to go help me run the 2002 trivia game?"

She thought about it, about Maggie's words, and her own fears and doubts. She reminded herself what was wise, but knew, in the end, her body was going to make the decision for her. She only had one more night with Seth. What kind of fool would she be to leave before building up another supply of memories to last her the rest of her life?

"Okay," she told him, putting her hand in his. "Let's go."

# 5

ALTHOUGH SETH HAD THOUGHT the carnival idea was a stupid one, he and Lauren ended up having a great time. It was set up in a pretty meadow below the resort, and came complete with rides, cotton candy and stuffed animals. They manned their booth for a couple of hours, meeting a ton of people from their own graduating class, as well as from other schools. Then, once the next shift arrived, they strolled the grounds, hand in hand, eating corn dogs, riding rides and chatting with old friends. Many people remembered them as a couple, most remembered prom night and all looked surprised to see them so…friendly.

Hell, he couldn't deny it, he was surprised himself. This weekend had gone better than he'd ever dreamed it would. Lauren was back in his life, and he wasn't letting her get away again. He didn't give a damn about geography or their jobs or what their friends or family thought. He'd lost her once, and it had crushed him for a decade. No way was he up for a second round of such misery.

"How about going on the Ferris wheel?" he asked, eyeing the brightly colored ride that rose above the midway. It wasn't huge, not like the ones in theme parks, but was pretty tall given the private location of this event.

She resisted. "I don't know…"

"Oh, come on, don't be a chicken."

She elbowed him in the ribs, then followed him to the ride. They waited in line, got into a swinging seat and held hands as it began to ascend. The countryside was in full summer bloom, green and hilly, and the late-afternoon sunshine made everything gleam with soft light. But they didn't spend much time looking at the landscape. Because as soon as the seat swung off the loading platform and lifted them out of sight of the others on the ground, Seth turned to her and covered her mouth in a hungry kiss.

She kissed him back, shifting as much as she could, dangling one leg over his. It had only been hours since she'd left his bed, but he'd missed her like hell, and needed to claim her again.

If this had been one of those Ferris wheels with the large, closed-in compartments, he might have done more than kiss her.

When they finally broke apart, she smiled at him. "I'm a little dizzy."

"From the ride?"

"Yeah, that's it."

"Same here."

They laughed together, tilting until their foreheads met and he was looking down at their hands, clasped together on his lap. Though he wasn't sure she was ready to hear it, or would believe it, he couldn't wait any longer to tell her how he felt.

"I love you, Lauren."

She stiffened, her fingers clenching. He didn't let her go, squeezing tighter.

"I mean it. I've always loved you."

The ride stopped as someone got off or on far below. They were swinging high above the carnival grounds, the earth spread out below them, just, as he thought their future was. Limitless, beautiful. Filled with possibility.

"You shouldn't say that," she finally replied, her voice soft, tight. She pulled her hands away and moved her leg until she was sitting stiffly beside them. "You can't mean it."

"Of course I mean it," he insisted, not sure whether she was being serious, or she truly was retreating from him—from the declaration he thought she'd be glad to hear.

"That's ridiculous."

The first time he'd told a woman he loved her, she called him ridiculous. Nice. "Gee, thanks."

She turned her head and looked at him, and he saw the moisture in her eyes and the way she couldn't stop nibbling on her bottom lip. "Seth, we were kids. We haven't seen each other in ten years."

"You know what they say," he replied, trying to keep his tone light, trying to understand why she hadn't immediately admitted she loved him, too, when he knew she did. "Absence makes the heart…"

"Forget."

He snorted. "Not even close."

He couldn't forget her if he tried. He would remember her face, her voice, her touch, even on his deathbed.

The ride started moving again, and as they swept toward the bottom, he was surprised to see Lauren signal to the operator that she wanted off.

Okay, this wasn't just nerves. She wasn't being shy or coy. Something was seriously wrong.

He didn't want to confront her about it here, in front of all these people, so he followed her off the ride in silence, then took her arm to weave through the crowds. They left the carnival grounds, heading up the slope to the hotel. But rather than heading for the door, he steered her toward a side lawn, where he'd seen a gazebo.

She let him lead her there. Once they were inside, where he was sure they were alone and wouldn't be interrupted, he said, "Tell me what's wrong."

She wouldn't meet his eye. "Nothing's wrong, Seth. It's been wonderful. You just…you don't have to tell me you love me to make me feel better about sleeping with you. I don't have any regrets."

His jaw fell. "You think I… Wait, you seriously think I was handing you some kind of 'it was great baby, maybe I'll call you' line?"

She finally looked up at him, slowly shaking her head. "No, I know you weren't." Lifting a hand to his chest, until her fingertips rested right over his pounding heart, she continued. "I think you're caught up in the past, confusing it with the present."

She was his past. And his present. If only she would see it.

"This place is designed to do that, to make you travel back in time emotionally, if not physically," she said. "We finally got the night we wanted, and you said the words you think you would have said then, even though the time and circumstances are completely different."

"Don't tell me what I feel," he snapped, suddenly growing angry.

"Seth, you don't even know me anymore." She sounded weary, sad. "You were a teenage boy, I was the girl who got away. You've romanticized me in your mind. That's all."

He stepped back, feeling as though he'd been slapped. She really was accusing him of never loving her, when all he'd thought of for years was how much he'd give to have her in his life again.

"You're wrong," he told her.

Then, knowing one way he could prove it, he reached into his back pocket, drawing out a handful of faded, worn-looking envelopes. "These are for you. I had planned to give them to you later, so we could have a laugh over what a sappy kid I was. Now…hell, read them, keep them, trash them. Do what you want. But don't ever tell me I don't know how I feel."

Not trusting himself to say anything else, or to even look at her, for fear he'd make things worse, he spun on his heel and stalked out of the gazebo, leaving Lauren alone.

Maybe she'd read his letters—the ones he'd written to her over the years—and maybe she wouldn't. Either way, he'd given it his best shot. The ball was in her court.

LAUREN STOOD IN THE GAZEBO for a long time after Seth had gone, wondering how things could have gone so suddenly wrong. They'd been having a wonderful day. He'd been sexy and charming, she'd been happy and carefree.

Then he'd told her he loved her…and she'd turned into a hard-hearted bitch.

She just couldn't stop thinking about what she and Maggie had been talking about at breakfast. About how it couldn't possibly be love, not after all this time, not based on a teenage romance.

"But what if it is possible?" she mumbled, not sure who she was asking.

She had loved Seth ten years ago, she knew that for sure. And she had continued to love him for a lot of years after he'd left, even when she'd tried desperately to hate—or at least forget—him.

And now?

"I still love him."

Truthfully, she'd never stopped.

But could a guy really be the same? Could their relationship have meant as much to him as it had to her? She'd always known Seth was special—that he had heart and character. Still, could he have loved her with the kind of real, lasting love that endured separation and time?

She glanced down at the stack of pages in her hand, curious about what he'd left her. Seeing several envelopes with her name on them, she walked to the bench and sat down, more curious than ever. She recognized Seth's handwriting on the outside, and her own old address in Chicago. But these letters weren't postmarked, they'd never been mailed.

She opened the top one, and pulled out a piece of notebook paper covered in Seth's sloppy, teenage handwriting. It was dated May 2002. Right after he'd disappeared.

Every word in it broke her heart.

Tears rose in her eyes as she read his story, in his own hand, his own writing, told while it was still going on. He'd been confused, furious, afraid and lonely. And missing her. Oh, how he'd missed her.

How he'd loved her. He said so, again and again, with every tender phrase, every tender reminiscence of things they'd done, every wish for a moment they'd never shared—and he'd feared they never would.

"Oh, God, Seth," she whispered, tears falling down her cheeks as she finished the letter and reached for the next one. And the one after that.

There were seven in all, and they spanned a period of several years. The first had been written in South America. The last in L.A. just eighteen months ago. Even after he'd thought she'd refused to contact him, that he'd never see her again, he'd still written, as if she were his conscience and his confessor…and his long lost love.

She watched him grow up, watched him age, his handwriting maturing, his messages going from angry but hopeful to melancholy and resigned. He'd truly thought he would never see her again, and that she would never read these words, so he'd felt free to pour out his heart on the page.

And every word, every letter, told all the same story: he loved her. He'd always loved her, with the kind of real, mature, lifelong love she'd been telling herself he couldn't possibly have felt.

She should have known better than to compare Seth Crowder to any other guy—or man—she'd known. He was unique, always had been, and she'd done him a genuine disservice in forgetting that, even for a few hours.

She had never felt more awful about herself than she did at that moment.

"Lauren? Is that you?"

Looking up, she spied a very attractive young woman with curly brown hair and big green eyes. It took her only a second before those eyes became familiar and the curve of the cheek did, as well. "Emily," she said, rising to her feet, clutching Seth's letters.

"Are you okay?" Seth's sister asked, stepping into the gazebo. She obviously saw the tears Lauren hadn't wiped away. "What happened?"

"I've been really stupid," she said between sniffles. Then, thinking the worst, she asked, "Did you come to tell me Seth's leaving?"

Emily came over and draped an arm across her shoulder, offering Lauren comfort and support, the way Lauren had offered it to her when she'd been a little girl. "Of course not. He got roped into helping with the slide show at the dance so he's in the banquet room setting up."

"Oh, thank God. I need to talk to him."

Emily didn't let her go. "I think you need to go dry your tears first. And maybe get ready for the dance. I have a little something for you to wear to it."

Hearing the mischievous tone in the younger woman's voice, Lauren raised a curious brow.

"Come on, I'll help you get ready."

SETH REALLY HAD NO DESIRE to go to the "reunion formal" that night. What he wanted to do was find Lauren, get her alone and make her at least admit the possibility that he wasn't such a shallow jerk, that he could actually still love her after all these years. That he'd loved her then.

That she loved him.

But she wasn't answering her phone in her room, nor did she open the door when he knocked. He'd gone back out to the gazebo, but hadn't seen her there, either. Finally, he'd checked with Em and made sure she hadn't left altogether. Honestly, if she had, he didn't know what he would have done. Maybe borrowed Em's car, driven to Chicago to her parents' house and pounded on the door until someone let him in?

In the end, though, when his sister assured him Lauren would be showing up at tonight's dance, he just waited. He went to his room and took a shower before dressing in the tux he'd brought along for tonight's formal event.

Heading back toward the elevator, he paused at her door, listening for any noise from inside her room. He heard nothing. She was either lying low, or was already gone. Either way, she obviously wasn't ready to see him.

Cursing under his breath, he went downstairs and headed for the correct ballroom. It was already crowded, filled with guys in suits or tuxes and women in glittery dresses or gowns. Not exactly prom style, a little more mature, but with a familiar air of desperate longing to create a night worth remembering.

He stepped inside, and was swallowed by the crowd. He smiled and nodded, looking around every person he met, trying to find a familiar brunette with gold streaks in her hair.

Finally, just when he'd given up hope of finding her, he heard someone nearby gasp.

"Oh, my God, is that Lauren? What's she doing?"

Spinning around, he saw the woman who'd spoken gaping toward the front of the room, where a stage had been set up for a few speakers and awards to be presented later. All around him, everyone else turned their attention there, too. A few people laughed, most smiled and almost every one turned to find Seth in the crowd.

Then that crowd melted away, parting to clear a space between him and the stage. A spotlight settled on it, landing on the woman who stood there, all alone.

"Lauren," he breathed.

She wore a long gown, pink, the color appropriate for the girl she had been, but the slinky cut was all sexy, sultry woman. It clung to her, descended in a deep V over her breasts, skimmed over her hips, was slit high on the thigh and fell to the floor in a glimmering wave.

But that wasn't all she wore.

On her head was a flimsy crown, like something a little girl would wear at a princess birthday party. It was silver, with a big jeweled heart on the front.

And over her dress, she wore a paper sash with the words *Prom Queen: 2002* carefully stenciled on it. And in her hands, she held another crown…apparently, *his*.

Seth began to smile. Then to laugh.

His heart nearly bursting from his chest, he strode through the crowd, his eyes glued to her smiling face. Nearby, someone started to clap, then someone else. Applause rolled through the crowd, and the clapping was soon accompanied by whistles and cheers.

"Get her, Seth!"

"About damn time!"

He ignored them all, conscious of nothing but Lauren, who watched him approach, not moving, never shifting her gaze off his face. Love shone off every inch of her.

He got to the stage, put a hand on the edge and vaulted up

onto it, ignoring the steps on the side. It would take too damn long to get to them.

"You came," she said.

"I'm sorry I'm so late."

"It's never too late."

She stepped closer, lifting the plastic crown. Seth tipped his head forward and let her place it on his head. Smiling, they turned to face the crowd, who whooped and cheered for their finally crowned together prom king and queen.

The applause was still thundering, but Seth needed to hold her close, to convince himself this was really happening. He swept her into his arms and their mouths came together in a warm, tender kiss. They made all the declarations, the apologies, the promises in silence. Then they drew apart and made them verbally.

"I love you, Seth," she said, her voice unshaking and sure. "And I'm so happy you still love me."

"You believe that now?"

She nodded, solemn, accepting what he'd been trying to tell her. She'd owned his heart for more than a decade. He'd never loved anyone else, and never would. It was Lauren or nobody.

"So, would you like to dance?" he asked, noting they were already swaying to some internal music only they could hear.

"I'd love to."

"And would you like to come home with me to California?"

"That, too."

He squeezed her, kissing the tip of her nose, and whispered, "One last thing…"

He lowered himself to one knee. Their former classmates went wild. Tears formed in Lauren's blue eyes and spilled down her cheeks.

"Would you like to marry me?"

Lauren didn't hesitate; she dropped to her knees in front of him. "Oh, God, yes, Seth, I'd like that very much."

The roar was deafening, but he couldn't hear anything except her voice, couldn't see anything but her beautiful, smiling face, her mouth forming the word *yes*.

Maybe her family would object. Maybe they still had a lot of logistics to work out. Maybe they were crazy and impulsive.

But it didn't matter. This was meant to happen. It always had been.

He had her now. And he was never letting her go.

\* \* \* \* \*

# JANELLE DENISON

## CAN'T GET YOU OUT OF MY HEAD

To my Plotmonkey pals, Leslie Kelly and Julie Leto.
I'm so happy that we were finally able
to write this anthology together.

And to Don. It's been thirty years this month since
the day we met. I love you more now than ever!

# 1

WILL BECKMAN STARED AT the e-invitation he'd received for his ten-year high school reunion, his finger hovering over the delete button as he considered just how great it would be if he could obliterate four painful, torturous years in high school as if they'd never happened just by erasing the email. Being an accredited computer geek, he ought to create an app for that, because he was pretty damn sure he wasn't the only high school graduate who wanted to forget those awkward years.

The truth was, he had no desire to go back in time and revisit classmates who'd treated him like an outsider because he'd been a quiet nerd who'd been more interested in science and computers than sports and partying. The rich, cool kids had looked down their noses at him and talked behind his back about the out-of-date secondhand clothes he'd worn. And being a general misfit had made him the target for the jocks and bullies who thought it was cool to insult and intimidate the little guys who had more brains than brawn.

Over the course of four long years, he'd been pushed and shoved, taunted and teased mercilessly, and suffered physical and emotional abuse from a good percentage of his peers. The day he'd graduated, he felt as though he'd been released from prison, and the freedom had been liberating.

College, thank God, had been much easier to get through. In fact, it had even encouraged his interest in computer programming, HTML coding and software development. The one thing that had separated him from the cool kids back in high school had been his salvation, his lifeline and the road map to his success while attending the University of Illinois where he'd majored in computer science.

By the time he'd graduated at the age of twenty-two, he'd created a complex and sophisticated software program designed to encrypt and protect online data and block identify theft—all from a small desk and laptop in the corner of his dorm room. Now, he and over two dozen employees occupied an entire floor in a cushy Chicago high-rise where his security-based company, Sentinel, provided services to some of the biggest name brand businesses in the world. And their clientele was growing daily.

Still, for some strange reason, he wasn't ready to completely discard the invitation to the reunion just yet. He leaned back in his plush leather chair and stared out the plate-glass window behind his desk, taking in the spectacular view of Lake Michigan.

He definitely felt a sense of satisfaction in what he'd accomplished in such a short period of time, and how much he'd changed along the way. Being the CEO of his own company had given his confidence a huge boost and elevated his personal status in the business world.

He was no longer the lanky, quiet kid who wore glasses and braces, the one who shied away from confrontation or difficult situations. Now, he was a multimillion-dollar business professional who garnered respect in the industry and had accumulated dozens of awards and accolades for his insight and ingenuity. He'd appeared in *Forbes* magazine, had been named as one of the top ten young entrepreneurs by

*Business Week* and had landed on the top twenty-five list for the Fastest-Growing Tech Companies.

Life was good and far surpassed the impoverished way he and his three older sisters had grown up. He honestly couldn't care less what his classmates thought of him now. He had absolutely nothing to prove to anyone. But there was one person he hadn't been able to forget in the past ten years: pretty, blond-haired, green-eyed Ali Seaver, who had the face of an angel and a curvaceous body designed to drive a hormonal teenage boy crazy with lust. That explained his reluctance to hit the delete button on the invite.

Ali had been the captain of the cheerleading squad, homecoming queen and all-around social extrovert. She was his opposite in almost every way, and so far out of his league he was certain she'd never give a computer geek like him a chance. But that hadn't stopped him from watching her from afar, thinking about her, and fantasizing about what it would be like to date a girl like her. Then one day fate had intervened.

When her wealthy parents had hired him to tutor Ali for an entire month in preparation of her senior final in calculus, the one class in which she struggled to maintain her grades, he'd been nervous and self-conscious. But unlike most of the popular girls who wouldn't give him the time of day, Ali had been friendly and sweet. She'd treated him as an equal and made him feel comfortable. The awkwardness he'd been anticipating had been nonexistent between them and they just *clicked*.

Beyond the learning, beyond the studying, they'd gradually started talking about personal things and discovered they had a lot in common, such as their love of reading classic novels and watching old Hitchcock movies. He learned she had a weakness for cherry Life Savers, that her favorite place to explore was the Museum of Contemporary Art and that she *hated* how guys stared at her well-developed chest instead of looking her in the eye when she talked to them.

Luckily for Will, he had three older sisters who'd trained him to treat women with respect. And yeah, that meant *not* staring at a girl's breasts, no matter how instinctive that particular temptation was.

Ali had shyly admitted that she thought he was cute. She'd easily coaxed smiles and laughter out of him, and she'd made him feel hopeful. Of course, he'd fallen head over heels in love with her, though as an adult, he knew his emotions had been nothing more than infatuation. At the end of their last tutoring session he'd given in to the urge to kiss her, and to his shock, she'd kissed him back. Even now, ten years later, thinking about that moment between them made his stomach tighten with desire.

Feeling higher than a kite after that first kiss, he'd asked her out on a date, despite knowing that her friends thought he was beneath her socially. Much to his surprise, she'd gone against peer expectations and said *yes*.

Will's excitement had been short-lived. Tim Delgado, the linebacker for the football team, threatened him with a whole lot of pain and humiliation if he didn't break things off with Ali. Though he was mortified to admit it now, he'd been petrified, especially since he'd been on the receiving end of Tim's brute strength before. Two hours before his date with Ali, he'd canceled, giving her no explanation beyond the fact that he'd changed his mind and was no longer interested in her. All lies.

*Christ,* he thought with a shake of his head. The cheerleader and homecoming queen had more guts than he had back then.

Will blew out a harsh, agonized breath and rubbed a hand along his jaw, remembering with too much clarity how obviously confused she'd been over his blatant rejection, how hurt she'd sounded on the phone. From that day on, he'd ignored Ali at school, avoided any kind of contact with her when she tried to approach him, and eventually she started ignoring him, too.

At the end of the school year when the yearbooks were released and the "Most Likely To" candidates were announced, Ali Seaver had been voted the Girl Most Likely to Become a Playboy Bunny. And in a cruel joke meant to demoralize Will, he'd been dubbed the Guy Most Likely to Date a Playboy Bunny...NOT. He had no doubt, then or now, who'd been responsible for the deliberate insult.

God, he still harbored so many regrets about what he'd done to Ali, when all she'd done was be nice to him. And he sure as hell harbored his share of "what-ifs."

He wondered if she was attending the reunion. Once the thought was in his head, he couldn't contain his curiosity. Turning his chair back around, he clicked on the link in the email invite that led to the RSVP site for the weekend get-together. He found Ali's name and checked on her status. She'd clicked on Yes to attend and wasn't bringing a guest.

His heart thudded in his chest. This was it, he thought. His one chance to see her again. Maybe he would even make amends, telling Ali the truth of what happened ten years ago—if she'd even talk to him. She might choose to ignore him, but he refused to allow it. He was no longer the quiet, insecure teenager he'd once been. He was confident of who he was as a man, self-assured enough to handle her reaction and have his say. And maybe have something more.

He'd felt something for Ali back then. He wondered if he'd feel something for her now. One way or another, he intended to find out.

Decision made, he checked Yes. This was going to be interesting....

# 2

ALI SEAVER FOLLOWED her best friend, Renee Griffen, into their ten-year high school reunion's welcome reception at the Celebrations resort. The two of them were fashionably late, and the cocktail party was already in full swing, their class-mates mingling and getting reacquainted with drinks in hand.

She inhaled a deep, fortifying breath, unable to quell the nervous little quiver in her stomach. Not because she was about to connect with old friends she hadn't talked to in nearly ten years, but because the one guy she thought she'd never see again had confirmed his attendance for the weekend.

She'd been more than a little shocked to see Will Beck-man's name on the reunion roster. Judging by the conversa-tions they'd had during that short period when he'd tutored her, she knew that Will didn't have a whole lot of warm and fuzzy high school memories he'd want to revisit ten years later. Having followed his huge success as an internet entre-preneur who had a personal net worth in the multimillions, she wondered if maybe he was returning to thumb his nose at all those people who'd made his high school years so misera-ble. Not that she'd blame him, after all the abuse he'd suffered.

But knowing that he was going to be here tonight, for the weekend possibly, stirred emotions in Ali that should no longer exist by now, along with that ten-year-old question she'd pondered way too often: What had she done to make Will reject her so completely?

Back then, she'd been ashamed to admit that a small part of her had been relieved when he'd ended things before she'd gotten any more attached to him. As soon as word had spread that the two of them were going on a date, she'd become the center of gossip, none of it pleasant. People she'd thought were her friends, including most of the girls on the cheerleading squad, had not only treated her like an outcast, but their catty, hurtful remarks and the rude way they'd deliberately whispered behind her back had given Ali a taste of the kind of torment Will dealt with on a regular basis.

It was ridiculous to let a teenage-girl-crush-gone-wrong be anything more than a blip on her radar, but she couldn't deny that the entire incident still bothered her. She'd been raised not to judge people, to accept them at face value, and there had been so much about Will to like once she'd really got to know him. But for her, being so guileless and trusting had caused her a whole lot of pain and heartache. Will had burned her once, her ex-fiancé had burned her twice and now she was far more cautious when it came to guarding her emotions.

Standing on the fringes of the party with Renee, she recognized many faces, but had no desire to approach anyone in particular. After graduating high school, the people she'd hung out with had all gone their separate ways, to different colleges, working full-time and generally making new lives for themselves. Eventually, she'd lost touch with those classmates, all except for Renee, who'd been her very best friend since first grade, and had remained steadfast and true during that senior year debacle.

With the popularity of Facebook and other social networking sites, she'd reconnected with old classmates, but their interaction was all superficial. She'd gotten glimpses of their lives now, who was married with families, who was single and or divorced, and what line of work some had chosen. But she didn't really *know* these people any longer, or what, if anything, they had in common except what had happened in the past.

Ali glanced at Renee, who was eagerly scanning the crowd for a certain someone. "Tell me again why I agreed to come to this shindig?" Because she was quickly regretting the decision.

"You're my backup plan, just in case things don't work out with my old flame," Renee reminded her, flashing Ali one of her gregarious grins.

"Oh, yeah, I almost forgot," Ali replied with wry humor. "This weekend is all about *you* getting laid."

Renee had spent the past few months hooking up long-distance via phone calls and Skype with Jake Copeland, the guy she'd lost her virginity to back in high school. The experience had been quick and totally unsatisfying. This weekend was all about a fun, sexy "do-over," and if things didn't work out with Jake, Renee knew she could use Ali as an excuse to end the encounter early.

Her friend was dressed to impress, in a skintight, strapless bandage dress that made Ali's outfit—slim black pants and a loose boatneck blouse that was stylish, yet minimized her voluptuous breasts—look downright modest in comparison. The dark emerald color hugged Renee's body, and complemented her green eyes and natural auburn-hued hair perfectly.

"You jealous that I'm getting some action this weekend?" Renee asked, her tone playful.

Ali laughed and shook her head. "No. Not at all."

"You should be." Renee sighed, and Ali knew exactly what was coming next. "It's been nearly two years since your breakup with Michael. It's time for you to get back on the horse, so to speak."

Yeah, it was definitely time for her to start dating again, but it was a matter of finding someone *worth* opening herself up to again. "Well, that's not going to happen with anyone here at the reunion." Of that, she was absolutely certain.

"Ali and Renee, over here!"

They both turned toward the female voice who'd called their names. Leanne Barton, dressed in her signature hot pink outfit and big blond hair, was waving them over to a group of women Ali recognized as the girls who'd been on the cheer squad. The same ones who'd mocked her when they'd discovered she'd accepted a date with Will. Back then, she'd learned just how shallow and pretentious they could be, and hoped those qualities had changed for the better.

Even still, dread settled in her stomach like a rock, and she pasted on a bright smile as she moved forward with Renee. "And so it begins," Ali murmured beneath her breath. "If it wasn't for you being my best friend…"

"I know, I know. You wouldn't be here."

Once they reached their old friends, Leanne was quick to introduce her older-by-a-good-thirty-years husband, informing everyone that he was a plastic surgeon, and they were living a *fabulous* life in Beverly Hills. She flashed the huge diamond on her ring finger as they all talked, and just like old times, it was clear she still liked to be the center of attention.

The other women chatted about their lives, too. All of them had either married and had families, or had great careers. But then, so had she. Ali was a graphic artist with her own business, and Renee was a travel consultant for large corporate clients.

On the surface, everyone seemed to be living a charmed life, and once they were all caught up to date, the high school reminiscing began, with everything from talking about their favorite teachers, to parties they'd attended, to laughing about how Robbie Grant had gotten suspended for streaking naked through campus during lunch as a senior prank.

"And we certainly can't forget Ali's lapse in judgment when she accepted a date with nerdy Will Beckman," Lori Franklin said with a light laugh that did nothing to conceal the snark behind her comment. Snark had always been her forte. "Talk about high school social suicide. I can't imagine what you were thinking to do such a thing."

Ali was so shocked by Lori's mean-spirited remark, she didn't know what to say.

"Speaking of Will Beckman, I saw his name on the reunion roster," Courtney said, her eyes alight with sudden excitement. "He's supposed to be here tonight. I couldn't believe it when I saw him on the cover of *Forbes* about a year ago. He's this huge internet mogul."

"He's rich now?" Sudden and genuine interest infused Lori's voice.

"Oh, yeah. *Filthy* rich," Courtney confirmed with a nod. "A multimillionaire. And he's *single*."

"Sounds like he might have to be my second husband," the newly divorced Bridget Donohue said, sounding completely serious.

Ali listened to the conversation, disgusted and disappointed that the girls she'd hung out with in high school could still be so full of themselves. God, she needed a drink. A strong one to get her through the rest of the evening.

"There he is," Renee whispered from beside Ali.

Ali's pulse jumped in anticipation, and she glanced up, fully expecting to see Will—and quickly realized that Renee had just spotted Jake across the room, where he was talking with some classmates.

Renee grabbed her arm in concern. "Will you be okay if I leave you?"

No way was Ali going to ruin Renee's big plans. Ali was

a big girl, and she could handle being alone for the evening. "Go and have a good time."

A few minutes after Renee slipped away to be with Jake, Ali decided it was time for her to leave the group, too, and mingle with other less egotistical alumni. "I'm going to get myself a glass of wine," she said, the perfect excuse to move on.

"Hey, girls!" a loud male voice bellowed from behind Ali, waylaying her plan to politely slip away. "You're all looking mighty fine."

Knowing exactly who that voice belonged to, Ali briefly closed her eyes, wondering if her evening could get any worse. In the next instant, Tim Delgado stood beside her—the football team's star linebacker and the guy she'd dated for a very short time until she realized what a jackass he truly was the night of their senior prom.

While he chatted with the other women and drank from his bottle of beer, Ali cast him a sidelong glance, stunned by the considerable difference in his physical appearance. He'd once been a super-fit, good-looking star athlete who believed that he and his football friends ruled the school. After graduating, he'd headed off to Oregon State University where he'd received a full-ride football scholarship, until he'd blown out his knee his freshman year while trying to jump from a house rooftop into a swimming pool during a drunken frat party. From what she'd heard, the incident had ended any chance he might have had as a pro football player.

Now, she barely recognized Tim. His once lean and muscular body was replaced by a pot belly, full face and receding hairline. What *hadn't* changed was his loud and obnoxious personality, and that arrogant attitude that grated on her nerves. It didn't help matters that barely an hour into the cocktail reception, he already appeared to be intoxicated.

"Ali, Ali, Ali," Tim drawled, turning his attention her way

and giving her a blatant once over, his gaze stopping to leer at her chest in a way that felt like a personal violation. "The girl most likely to become a Playboy Bunny. I keep looking in my *Playboy* magazine every month, hoping to see you in there as the next centerfold." He smirked, as if his crude wisecrack should have flattered her.

She knew he'd been the one to nominate her for such an embarrassing title, and had taken the opportunity to humiliate Will in the process with a counter snub. *Ugh*. Now she just wanted to throw up—all over Tim. She was never going to last the entire weekend, and once she knew that things were good with Renee and Jake, Ali was going to cut the reunion short. Nobody would miss her, and she'd rather be at home working than subjecting herself to uncomfortable encounters with people she could no longer relate to. If she ever had.

"Oh. My. *God*." Lori's exaggerated tone, tinged with excitement and awe, replaced the awkward silence that had settled over the group after Tim's comment. "Look who's here."

Everyone glanced toward the entrance of the cocktail party and the tall, good-looking, dark-haired man standing there, intently surveying the crowd. Ali's breath caught in her throat, her heart skipped a beat or two and a shiver of pure awareness raced up her spine. *Oh, my God* was an understatement.

"Is that *nerdy* Will Beckman?" Leanne asked, her eyes wide with shock.

"I believe it is," Courtney said, licking her glossy lips as if someone had just offered her a juicy steak. "Who would have thought Will Beckman would turn out to be so freakin' *hot*."

Ali couldn't agree more. There wasn't anything remotely nerdy about Will's appearance now. At twenty-eight, he'd grown into his lanky body, his broad shoulders filling out his tailored suit coat to male perfection. His hips were still lean and narrow, but his thighs were more muscled, his stance confident and commanding. He no longer wore glasses, and his jaw was more defined, giving his handsome face an added dimension of sensuality. His rich brown hair, however, was very much the same—messy and a little unkempt, just the way she'd always liked it.

Clearly, the gawky computer geek had become a man. A self-assured, devastatingly sexy man. The transformation was unexpected, amazing and impressive. And it left her feeling both anxious and excited to see him.

Will's gaze came to a stop on her, and Ali's pulse rate accelerated. A faint smile tipped up one corner of his mouth, and he started toward their group, his stride decisive and determined.

"I get first dibs," Bridget said as she tugged the bodice of her dress down just a bit farther to display the swells of her breasts, then ran her fingers through her highlighted hair.

*Really?* Ali thought, suppressing the urge to roll her eyes at the absurdity of it all. Were these women still in high school? Will hadn't been good enough for any of them back then, but his looks and money now made him fair game. *Unbelievable.*

As Will neared, Tim downed the rest of his drink, then puffed out his chest, as if he was still the big man on campus and wanted to make sure everyone knew it. His gaze narrowed in on Will, and as soon as he came to a stop a few feet away from Ali, Tim didn't hesitate to open his big mouth and start causing trouble.

"So, did you come to the reunion to gloat about how rich you are?" the ex-football player asked in a disparaging tone.

Will didn't even glance Tim's way, his vivid blue eyes, still the deep, warm color of the Pacific Ocean, remaining locked on Ali. "No. I'm only here for one reason."

"Can't imagine what that would be," Tim continued, letting out a sarcastic laugh. "You have nothing in common with any of us."

"I came to see Ali." Will smiled at her, and Ali went weak in the knees.

Tim made a grunting sound. "That's pretty damned ballsy after the way you dumped her the end of senior year. What makes you think she'd have anything to do with you now?"

A muscle in Will's cheek flexed, the only indication that Tim's spiteful words had any kind of impact on him. Ali couldn't believe Tim's offensive behavior, but it was quickly becoming clear that he was threatened by Will's good fortune and was trying to downplay his own insecurities and failures. Because while Tim's plans for a bright and promising future as a pro athlete had been crushed by his own stupidity, Will had succeeded in a big way. And Tim obviously couldn't handle knowing the underdog had become the top dog.

But instead of engaging in a war of words with Tim, Will took the high road and kept his cool, and his focus on Ali. "Why don't we let Ali decide how she feels about me being here."

Something odd was going on between Tim and Will, an undercurrent of antagonism she didn't understand. But there was one thing she knew for certain—her attraction to Will was still as strong and overwhelming as it had been in high school. He'd come to the reunion for the sole purpose of seeing her, and she was curious to know why.

Then she caught both Bridget's and Lori's envious expressions, and had to resist the urge not to laugh at the irony of it all. Instead, she met Will's expectant gaze and smiled. "I'm *very* glad to see you here, Will."

He exhaled, the relief on his face telling Ali just what her answer meant to him.

"That's all that matters to me." Will extended his hand toward her. "Care to join me for a drink?"

Unable to resist his invitation, she placed her fingers against his palm, willing to following him anywhere, because for the first time that night, she saw genuine interest in someone's eyes, instead of feigned enthusiasm. "I'd love to have a drink with you."

With her hand tucked securely in his, she walked with Will to the bar, fully aware that the two of them were about to be the center of gossip and speculation once again. Except this time, she honestly didn't care what other people thought of them being together. It felt good.

## 3

AT THE BAR, WILL ORDERED a Baileys on the rocks, and since Ali wasn't in the mood for hard liquor, she requested the same. Drinks in hand, they headed out the double French doors that gave way to a large, spacious patio with various places to lounge, along with heat lamps and fire pits to ward off the evening chill. Other alumni were gathered in groups outside, their laughter and conversation filling the night air, and Ali was glad when Will choose the farthest seating area away from the cocktail party and everyone else, where it was quiet and relatively secluded.

She sat down on the cushioned love seat situated in front of a low burning fire pit, and he settled in right beside her, so close that their thighs touched. The pressure was subtle, but made her very much aware of how alone they were, how intimate the setting was. Not that she was complaining. She felt more at ease with him than she did with anyone else back inside, and at the moment, there was nowhere else she'd rather be.

She took a drink of her cream liquor, enjoying the buttery toffee taste, with just a hint of whiskey. "I'm so sorry about what happened back there with Tim," she said, feeling the need to address the other man's surly disposition.

"You have nothing to apologize for." Will shrugged those well-developed shoulders of his. "Tim is…"

"An arrogant ass?" she supplied for him.

He chuckled lightly. The sound was deeper and richer than she remembered and created a bit of sensual havoc in the pit of her belly.

"I won't argue with that," he said, taking a drink before he continued. "Though I'm sure Tim has a lot of pent-up frustrations over what happened to him in college, not to mention the loss of his football career."

Will had never been one to bad mouth anyone, even if they deserved it, and that rare and genuine quality obviously hadn't changed. "Doesn't mean that it makes it okay to treat people rudely."

"What happened back there with Tim doesn't matter to me," he said, the confidence in his voice backing up his claim. "Like I said, the only reason I'm here is to see you. Nothing else matters."

The notion that he'd come to the reunion just for her gave Ali a little thrill. Okay, a *huge* thrill, but she managed to keep that bit of pleasure to herself. Because underneath it all, that cautious part of her couldn't stop wondering what his motivations were for wanting to see her again.

He stared at her face, the affection in his gaze unmistakable as he took in her features. "You look great, by the way." His voice dropped to a low, husky pitch, and he reached up, grazing the pad of his thumb along her jaw in a soft caress. "You were pretty at eighteen. Now, you're stunningly beautiful."

It was a bold move for someone who'd once been so shy around her, but she couldn't deny that this more assertive man attracted her all the more. Ali swallowed hard as his hand fell away, but the sensual warmth of his touch remained, creating a nice little buzz along her nerve endings that had nothing to do with the Baileys Irish Cream.

She smiled at Will, unable to remember the last time she'd received such a sweet, feel-good kind of compliment from a man. "You look great, too," she said, returning the sentiment.

"Yeah, amazing what ten years can do for a guy, huh?" His tone was wry. "Though I'm still not used to the whole suit and tie thing."

Maybe not, but he certainly looked good in one. Very polished and stylish. Like a man who finally felt comfortable in his own skin.

She took another long sip of her drink, watching Will over the rim of the glass, her curiosity getting the best of her. "After all this time, why would you come *here* of all places just to see me? You could have friended me on Facebook." She deliberately kept her voice light and teasing.

"Too clichéd," he said, a charming grin curving his full lips. "Everybody does the social networking thing these days. Me, I wanted to be original and actually talk to you, face-to-face. Though I have to confess, I did a Google search on you."

She laughed, glad to see that he still had that same quirky sense of humor she'd loved back in high school. "Did you find out anything I might not know about?"

He thought for a moment, the flickering flames from the fire pit casting a warm orange glow between them. "Well, I know that you started your own business doing personalized stationery and custom invitations and announcements, and you appear to be doing very well with it. You were very talented with your graphic art, and I'm glad to see you doing something you love."

Will had been one of the few people she'd shown her designs to back in high school. She remembered how impressed he'd been, and how he'd encouraged her to take more classes to make the most of her abilities. As an only child, she'd always had the support of her parents, no matter her endeavors, which made it so much easier for her to follow, and achieve, her true goals and dreams.

"Most of the orders and requests are internet based, but word of mouth and advertising have increased my business to the point that I'm completely self-sufficient," she said, setting her empty glass on a nearby table. "Last year, I was finally able to quit my full-time job and focus completely on Paper Bliss Designs." She was very proud of that.

Setting his glass next to hers, he stretched his arm along the back of the love seat, his fingers brushing oh-so-subtly along the bare skin at the base of her neck. "I also read that your fiancé left you standing at the altar," he said quietly.

She closed her eyes and groaned, feeling a sensation similar to being kicked in the gut. It looked like one of her most personal and private decisions had once made it into an article somewhere on the World Wide Web. Then again, she'd been engaged to a very prominent man, and the Chicago wedding had been a high-society event—until the morning of the wedding when Michael had called off the ceremony just before she was to walk down the aisle.

The very public rejection, along with the gossip that had ensued, had been painful to deal with and had initially touched on old insecurities. But while Michael's last-minute decision to stop the wedding had been devastating in that moment, in the long run she'd been grateful. It had been the right thing to do. For both of them.

Opening her eyes again, she rubbed her fingers across her brow and shook her head. "Wow, the internet is worse than being in high school. Just about everything is documented and archived, just to humiliate you forever."

He nodded in understanding. "Trust me, I feel your pain. I've tried to keep my personal life as private as possible, but the internet makes that difficult sometimes."

Most of what Ali had read online about Will had focused on his company, his many accolades and the fact that he was labeled as one of the youngest and richest bachelors in the internet world. She'd seen various pictures of him with beautiful women on his arm, but she'd never come across anything regarding him being in a committed relationship. However, that didn't mean he hadn't been seriously involved with someone in the past ten years.

Which brought her right back to the reason he was here at the reunion. "You still didn't answer my question," she said softly, meeting and holding his gaze steadily. "Why did you come here to see me?"

He exhaled a deep breath, and there was no mistaking the remorse that etched his handsome features. Gently grabbing both of her hands in his, he held them securely as he stared so deeply into her eyes she wondered if he could see into her soul. It certainly felt like it to her.

"I came here because you and I didn't part ways on the best of terms in high school," he said, stroking his thumbs across the back of her hands in a soothing caress, even though his voice had a rough edge to it. "With everything that happened at the end of our senior year, how things ended between us... Well, I have a whole lot of regrets, even now. There's so much I'd change if I had the chance to go back in time and do it all over again."

Oh, wow. The candor behind his words left no doubt in Ali's mind that he meant exactly what he'd just said. And it also compelled her to say something to ease his conscience. "We all do stupid things, Will. Especially as teenagers."

The frown furrowing his brow didn't ease. "I know, but I was *really* stupid, and I hurt you badly." He wove their fingers together, entwining them intimately. "I knew that then, and I wanted, no, *needed,* you to know how sorry I am for the way I treated you."

"Thank you," she said, realizing just how much she appreciated his honesty. "That means a lot."

If there was any shred of reservation left in her for what had happened in the past, his candid, heartfelt words wiped the slate clean. That he'd openly apologized and still felt bad about the incident after all these years said a lot about Will—about the upstanding, decent man he'd become, and possibly about how he still felt about her. Because who in their right mind would subject themselves to facing all the classmates who'd ridiculed him, just to make amends with a girl he'd once had a crush on if there wasn't still something there?

As for her, it was becoming increasingly clear that the attraction they'd once shared was still simmering between them, a small spark just waiting for the right tinder to turn it into a full-fledged wildfire. But there was suddenly an emotional component involved, all based on how he'd opened up to her, not knowing if she'd even accept his apology. That took guts and courage, and now that the olive branch had been extended, and accepted, a wealth of possibilities awaited the two of them. A second chance to see where all this might lead.

She visibly shivered as desire blossomed and spread through her veins in a heady rush, and Will mistook her reaction to a chill in the air. Releasing her hands, he shrugged out of his jacket to give to her.

"Here, take my coat," he said, then draped it over her shoulders, pulling it close around her body.

She really wasn't *that* cold, but he was so insistent she didn't want to refuse. And once his jacket settled around her, warm from his own masculine heat and smelling like his woodsy cologne, she didn't want to give it up.

"So tell me, how are you handling your major success?" she asked. They'd turned toward one another on the seat, and now his hand rested on her knee, which she didn't mind at all. His touch was both comforting and arousing. "Has a lot changed for you?"

"Everything's changed," he admitted, shaking his head as if even he couldn't believe how his life had turned out. "It's actually very surreal. I love what I do, especially when it comes to the programming part of the job, and I have to admit the money is obscene. But for me, it's not about being a millionaire and living a lavish, excessive lifestyle. I don't drive a fancy, high-dollar car. I don't live in a huge mansion. And I only have one vice—buying the latest and greatest electronic gadget to hit the market." His expression was sheepish, his grin boyishly sexy.

She remembered he'd taken on tutoring jobs in high school to not only help out financially with his family, but also to buy his first used laptop computer. They'd also had conversations about how Will's father had died when he was just a boy, and with four hungry mouths to feed, Will's mother had taken on two jobs to support the family, working over sixty hours a week. The Beckmans had struggled, but he'd never complained, not even when Ali knew he'd worn clothes from Goodwill because that's all his mother could afford, and ate peanut butter and jelly sandwiches on a daily basis.

"How is your mom doing?" she asked.

His eyes lit up, along with his smile. "She's doing amazingly well. She just got married to a great guy, they're both retired and travel a lot, and she's very happy." He stared at the fire pit for a moment, then met her gaze again. "The one thing all the money I've made has enabled me to do is to take care of my family, and I'm so grateful for that. The first thing I did when I had enough cash was buy my mom a new house, paid in full. And I've made sure that my sisters don't have anything to worry about, either."

She wasn't surprised to hear that Will's first priority was his family, or that he was still humble about his enormous success. He'd come from very frugal beginnings, and had become a man who knew how to save a dollar and spend it wisely, too.

"The one thing I've done that I'm extremely proud of is I started a program at Sentinel for teenagers who are having a hard time fitting in at high school and have an interest in computer software. If they have a strong GPA, I offer them an internship at the company, teach them about programming and software and give them a place where they're accepted and not bullied because they'd rather be tinkering with an HTML code than partying or playing sports."

Ali was content to listen to Will talk, impressed by the choices he'd made and how passionate he was about his company, and making a difference in the lives of kids who didn't easily fit in. He offered scholarships to various organizations, went to high schools to give speeches on keeping one's drive and focus on what mattered most to them, regardless of what anyone else thought. Will was a man who gave, and wanted nothing in return but to better the lives of those less fortunate—because he'd once been there himself.

For the next hour or so, their conversation ran the gamut of the past and present, giving them both better insight to the lives they'd led since high school. Their exchange was relaxed and comfortable, with laughter and flirtations, reminding Ali of how it had once been between the two of them ten years ago, before things had ended so painfully. And now, in just a matter of a few hours, she felt herself falling for him all over again. An exciting, scary prospect.

The fire in the pit had died down, and even cocooned in Will's jacket, she was starting to get a bit chilled. She suddenly noticed how quiet it was and glanced around, realizing everyone who'd been out on the patio earlier had gone inside. She had no idea what time it was.

"It's getting late, and colder," she said, even though she

was reluctant for them to part ways. "We should probably head back in."

He exhaled an exaggerated sigh and stood, then extended a hand to help her up. "If we must." He sounded just as disappointed.

She laughed, something that came very easily around him. "I know exactly how you feel." Placing her fingers against his warm palm, she let him pull her to her feet.

Once they were both standing, she expected Will to lead the way back to the party, but he didn't move. Face-to-face, with less than a foot of space separating them, she tipped her chin up and caught his serious expression. Then, she looked into his eyes, the same deep blue eyes she'd gotten lost in so many times as an infatuated teenage girl while he'd gone over her calculus homework with her. Now, she felt as though she were drowning in a sea of desire, and needed mouth-to-mouth resuscitation to survive how breathless he made her feel.

"God, I've missed that," he murmured, gently tucking a strand of her hair behind her ear before letting his fingertips trail sensuously along the shell of her ear, then down the side of her neck.

Deep inside, she trembled. The husky quality of his voice, combined with the heat in his gaze, completely and totally entranced her. "Missed what?" she asked, her own voice barely a whisper.

"The sound of your laughter. And especially *you*." He brazenly grazed the pad of his thumb along her lower lip, his gaze fixated on her mouth, which had parted on a sigh. "I was prepared for you to have changed, and you have, but all the wonderful qualities I fell so hard for ten years ago are still the same, just as I was hoping. Only now you're so much more vibrant. And sexy as hell."

Her body couldn't help but respond to his words. To him. Her pulse fluttered in her throat, and the breaths she managed to inhale were shallow. Each was filled with the warmth of him and the dark, enticing scent of his body, which had edged to within a tempting inch of her own.

His hands went to the collar of the suit jacket still draped over her shoulders, his fingers curling beneath the lapels and gently pulled forward, using those flaps as an anchor to draw her mouth closer to his, yet leaving her own hands unable to touch him. "Do you believe in second chances?" he asked, touching his lips to hers, ever-so-softly.

Her lashes drifted shut, and she managed, just barely, to stifle a needy moan. Because that's exactly what Will did to her. He made her want and yearn, and it had been forever since she'd been so thoroughly seduced. "Yes," she replied in a hushed tone.

He smiled against her lips. "Good. So do I."

Then, his mouth claimed hers, so confident and sure. He'd become a man who wasn't the least bit hesitant about taking what he wanted. His tongue swept inside, swirling slowly, seductively with her own, and pure pleasure rushed through her veins. He tasted like whiskey and toffee and the most delicious kind of sin.

Too soon, he lifted his head. His hot, hungry gaze—brimming with pure, undisguised lust—searched hers. "It's still there, isn't it?" he asked in awe.

"Oh, yeah," she rasped, knowing exactly what he meant. But this time around, the passion between them was stronger, more potent, more demanding.

Groaning deep in his chest, he released the lapels of his jacket and delved the fingers of one hand into her hair, and slid the other around her waist, bringing her flush against his hard thighs, his flat stomach and his muscular chest. Tangling his fingers through her blond waves, he angled her head and went in for another deep, thoroughly arousing kiss. Lips meshed, tongues mated and the erection making itself known against her belly only made the moment more heated and intense.

The hand he'd tucked beneath the coat skimmed over her hip and along her rib cage, leaving a trail of fire in its wake. He swept his thumb beneath the fullness of her right breast, and her nipples tightened painfully against the sheer lace of her bra. She made a small, wordless noise of approval, and he daringly cupped the fullness in his palm and teased the aching tip between his fingers.

She gasped into his mouth, but he continued to tempt and tease, his hips flexed against hers, making her feel wild and impulsive. She desperately wanted to be alone with him, preferably somewhere with a soft bed. The thought was shocking and spontaneous, especially for her, but all the signals were there, and there was no denying the instinctive way her body craved his. It was as if she'd been waiting the past ten years for him....

"Ali?" A high-pitched female voice called out from somewhere behind Will. "Ali, is that you?"

Startled out of her passionate haze, Ali jerked back, ending the kiss to end all kisses. Her face was still close to Will's, they were both breathing hard, and her cheeks felt flushed with desire—and soon-to-be embarrassment. As if realizing the compromising situation he'd put her in, his hands fell away from her hair and breast, though he didn't move away. He remained standing in front of her, shielding and protecting her, giving her a moment to catch her equilibrium, which she appreciated.

But that didn't stop Lori from invading their personal space. She came right up to the two of them, her eyes a bit glassy, most likely from too much alcohol.

"There you are, Ali," Lori said a little too loudly, a sly smirk playing across her lips as she glanced from Ali, to Will, then back to Ali again. "Sorry to interrupt whatever was going on, but we've been looking all over the place for you. The girls want to take a picture of the cheerleader squad, so we all have a 'then' and 'now' photo."

The last thing Ali wanted was to reminisce with people who were no longer friends, not when she wanted to spend that time with Will. But Lori didn't give her any choice. She looped her arm through Ali's and started tugging her toward the patio doors, and Ali knew she'd look like a bitch if she refused. A few pictures, then she was leaving the cocktail party with Will.

Except he wasn't following her. She stopped for a second, forcing Lori to do the same. "Aren't you coming inside?" she asked Will.

He sent her a warm, sexy smile and pushed his hands into the front pockets of his pants, reminding her that he most likely needed a little more time to cool down before being seen in public. "You go ahead."

"I'll be back," she assured him.

"Come on," Lori said, giving her arm an exasperated tug. "The girls are waiting."

And Lord forbid they keep the girls waiting, Ali thought with a roll of her eyes.

She dutifully posed for the pictures, forcing a smile while the other women laughed and cracked raunchy jokes that Ali didn't find funny at all. Oddly enough, she felt out of place, as if she didn't belong—and she was more than okay with that. There had been a time when she'd been popular, the young girl who had it all, but she knew that none of that mattered in the big picture of life. Especially *her* life.

Nearly twenty minutes later she was finally able to break away from the group, and she immediately headed back outside to the patio for Will. Except he wasn't there. She was definitely disappointed that he'd disappeared on her, but not at all disheartened.

Because a man didn't kiss a woman like Will had kissed her and not intend to follow through. At least she hoped that was his intention.

But old insecurities reared their head, reminding her of another time, and another place, when he'd left her waiting, and wanting. Only time would tell if history would repeat itself, if she was always destined to be the girl who got left behind.

# 4

WILL FINISHED THE LAST of his coffee as he shut down his laptop computer after reading emails and making sure there wasn't anything pressing he needed to take care of while he was gone. Since it was Saturday, all seemed quiet on the work front, but he always liked to be available to his clients, just in case anything required his attention.

Standing, he stretched his muscles, contemplating the day ahead. He'd woken up early that morning, spent an hour in the gym doing cardio, then ordered a light breakfast from room service while he'd taken a shower and changed. It was now eleven-thirty and the entire afternoon stretched ahead of him.

Feeling restless, he headed out the sliding glass doors to the patio overlooking one of the main pool areas, the Chicago summer heat already climbing into the high eighties. With his room on the twelfth floor, he had a wide view of the resort's impressive landscape and amenities. At Celebrations, there was definitely something for everyone, and it was a great place to have a reunion of any sort—if that was your sort of thing.

The only thing Will was interested in this weekend was Ali, and he was pretty certain he'd made those intentions clear last night.

Walking into his high school reunion's cocktail reception and ignoring everyone but Ali had been liberating. It didn't matter that people had stopped and stared at him, or whispered behind his back about how much he'd changed. Even the women had looked at him differently, with not-so-subtle interest in their eyes, but the only person's opinion he'd cared about was Ali's and she hadn't disappointed him. Their time together out by the fire pit, the talking, laughing and getting caught up on each other's lives, had bridged the gap between past and present, and reignited the connection they'd once shared.

And then there was that smoking-hot kiss to consider. He groaned even now, remembering how soft and warm she'd felt in his arms, how sweet and lush her mouth had tasted, how her full, firm breast had fit so perfectly in the palm of his hand. Her uninhibited response had nearly blown his mind, and if it hadn't been for Lori's untimely appearance, there was no telling just how far their make-out session would have gone.

As frustrating as the interruption had been, he'd been grateful for the distraction. Without it, he probably would have pulled Ali right back down to the love seat and who knows what would have happened? Sending her back into the reception had given him time to tamp down his arousal and clear his head. And it had given Ali time, too, to make sure that whatever happened next in their new, tentative relationship, she would be making the decision without the haze of desire clouding her judgment.

This weekend, he wanted no regrets between them. No lies or secrets or anything else to undermine the trust they needed to rebuild. And that meant finally confiding in Ali the true reason he'd severed their relationship back in high school. It wasn't a topic he was anxious to discuss with her, but it was necessary to clear the air and equally important for them to be able to start over fresh, without the past being any kind of bone of contention between them. And knowing that the desire was stronger than ever made it easy to pursue her, to do things right this time around.

The sound of people cheering, laughing and generally having fun drew his attention back down to the main pool, where a group of men and women were playing a game of volleyball in the water. He recognized most of the players from last night's reception. Two coed teams had squared off, and the game seemed to have taken on an aggressive, competitive edge with the men battling it out for the win, while trying to impress their bikini-clad teammates with their skills.

The volleyball game had been one of the many organized activities on today's agenda, along with an eighteen-hole game of golf, a hiking expedition, a scavenger hunt and a lesson in culinary cooking. There seemed to be something for everyone, and while he had no interest in any of those offerings because it meant making inconsequential small talk with people who'd once taunted him, he was curious which events Ali had opted for.

He didn't have to wonder for long. A woman exiting the hotel caught his eye, and he glanced in her direction, immediately recognizing Ali's silky blond hair and striking features, even though she was wearing a pair of sunglasses. She'd hidden the shape of her curves beneath a flowing purple thigh-length cover-up, and wore sandals on her feet. A large tote bag was slung over her shoulder and she picked up a towel from the attendant.

She was all alone, and his hands gripped the patio railing as he watched and waited to see where she was going. But instead of joining either the volleyball game or the other women lounging poolside, Ali slipped down a paved pathway that led to the resort's low-key lagoon, a place set aside for those who wanted more privacy and relaxation.

She disappeared from sight, but now that he'd seen where

she'd gone, he knew exactly how he was going to spend his afternoon. Heading back into his room, he changed into a pair of swim trunks, slipped into a pair of flip-flops and made his way to the lagoon. The pathway gave way to a lush, tropical area, surrounded by rock formations, crystal-blue water and even a few waterfalls. Where the main pool area was high energy, this place was tranquil and pure Zen. And best of all, he didn't recognize anyone from his reunion.

He spotted Ali reclining on a lounge chair across the way, her sunglasses perched on top of her head, the upper half of her body shaded by a large palm tree, and her long, bare legs soaking up the sun's warm rays. She was totally engrossed in the e-reader she held in her hand.

He started toward her, enjoying the few moments he had to take in the tantalizing vision of Ali in a two-piece bathing suit. Black and trimmed in gold, the top and bottom accentuated her feminine curves in all the right ways. While her choice of swimwear was modest compared to the other micro-string bikinis and thongs that covered just the bare essentials he'd seen at the main pool, he much preferred a suit that left a little to the imagination. Like Ali's.

But there was still a helluva lot of creamy skin exposed for his admiration. As he neared, his mouth went dry as dust as he thought about running his hands up her slender legs and supple thighs, feeling them tremble beneath his flattened palms. Her belly was flat and toned…and pierced with a dangling crystal sunflower, hinting at a bit of a naughty side to her good-girl personality. Her full breasts were completely covered by her halter-style top, but there was no denying she had a gorgeous rack, the kind that deserved to be worshipped with the caress of his fingers, the heat of his mouth, the stroke of his tongue over the pert nipples he'd felt beneath her bra last night.

Before his imagination caused the lower half of his body

to rise to the occasion, he shut off those lustful thoughts and stopped besides Ali's chair. "Hey, there."

She'd been so lost in the book she was reading that she didn't hear his approach and glanced up at him in startled surprise. "Oh, hi!"

"Hi, yourself." He grinned down at her, deliberately keeping his gaze above her neck. From what he could tell, other than a bit of gloss on her lips, she wore no makeup, and she was still beautiful, her skin flawless. "Enjoying the day?"

"I am." Her eyes, the color of rich moss, held a hint of reserve. "How about you?"

"I am now," he said, making it very clear she was the reason his day had just gotten brighter. "Mind if I join you?"

That wariness remained. "Um, sure. I guess."

Her response was less than enthusiastic, and after last night, he was expecting a more welcoming reception. Taking his cue from her, and hoping to hell he'd misread the whole situation, he offered her an easy way out. "If you want to be alone, I completely understand."

She hesitated a moment, then clearly relaxed. "No, sit down. Really. I want you to," she assured him and waved a hand toward a nearby lounge chair. "I just didn't know what to expect after the way you ditched me last night." She bit her bottom lip uncertainly.

He resisted the urge to smack himself in the head when he realized the thoughts that must have gone through her head. Yeah, leaving last night without an explanation might not have been the best decision on his part, especially after the way he'd rejected her back in high school. It probably felt like déjà vu for her.

"Ali, I didn't ditch you," he said, his tone emphatic. He never meant for her to think he'd blown her off. "*Ditching* implies I didn't want to be with you. And that's the furthest from the truth."

She set her e-reader aside, still not looking completely convinced. "Then why did you leave?"

He dragged the chaise close to her chair and sat down, deciding that the truth was the simplest, and easiest, explanation. "I knew if we spent any more time together, I wouldn't be able to keep my hands to myself."

Her face flushed from the sexy overtone of his words, but she appeared relieved to know his reasons for leaving her had been honorable. "Okay, fair enough. Though I don't think that would have been a bad thing."

"Good to know," he said, and chuckled, glad to know she wasn't opposed to more kissing, and touching, and other things.

In full view of the sun, he pulled off his T-shirt and settled more comfortably on the lounge chair, unable to miss the appreciative look in Ali's eyes as her gaze dropped below *his* neck. Not that he minded. As an adolescent, he'd been tall and gangly. Thank God he'd filled out over the years. He still wasn't into sports, but he did enjoy strength training and cardio, and that had gone a long way in defining muscles and developing his build.

"How come you're not out doing one of the many planned activities for today?" he asked.

"Organized events aren't my thing." She shrugged, the movement causing her breasts to bounce oh-so-enticingly.

Yeah, he *looked*. He was male, for crying out loud, and it was impossible not to appreciate those twin works of art. "I know what you mean," he agreed, quickly switching his gaze back up to her face, because lingering for more than a few seconds stepped over the line to ogling. "I'm more of a one-on-one kind of guy."

A slow, sultry smile curved up the corners of her mouth. "You do one-on-one very well."

Her flirtatious tone and the insinuation in her words shot

heat straight to his groin. "So, no golf or game of bikini Twister for you?"

She shuddered at the mention of the latter. "Bikini Twister is a just a little too up close and personal for me, especially with people I don't care to be up close and personal with. I'm very happy just to relax for the day. In fact, I even scheduled a hot stone massage and facial for this afternoon."

"Nice." He tipped his head curiously at her. "By the way, I thought I saw your best friend's name on the roster. Is Renee here at the reunion?" If she was, Will wondered why Ali wasn't spending her free time with her friend.

"Yes, she came to the reunion, but not to hang out with old classmates," she said, answering his silent question. "Do you remember her old boyfriend, Jake Copeland?"

The name was familiar, and he thought for a moment until the recollection settled in. "Yeah, Jake was in my English lit class our senior year." He'd also been one of the few guys who had been decent to Will.

"That's who she's with all weekend long. The two of them reconnected a few weeks ago online and decided to meet up here." Ali grinned, obviously happy for her friend. "Renee didn't make it back to our room last night, so I'm assuming everything is going well between her and Jake."

"Good for them," he said, just as a poolside waiter came up to them and delivered a small tray of fruit with some kind of dip and a glass of iced tea for Ali, which she must have ordered before he'd arrived.

"I'm happy to share my fruit with you," she said as she signed the receipt for the items. "Would you like something to drink?"

He shook his head and told the waiter, "I'm fine right now, thanks."

Once the guy was gone and they were alone again, she picked up a strawberry and dipped the tip into some kind of white, fluffy concoction. Will watched her take a bite, closing her eyes and moaning as she chewed. When her lashes fluttered back open, she looked like she'd just experienced ecstasy.

"Oh, my God," she groaned. "This is the sweetest, juiciest strawberry I've *ever* had." She picked up another and immersed it in the creamy dip. "Here. You *have* to try one," she said, offering him a bite.

While he could have taken the fruit from her and eaten it himself, he went with the spontaneous urge to grasp her wrist and tugged her hand up to his mouth. He took a bite of the strawberry, which smeared the delicious, marshmallow cream dip onto her fingers, giving him the perfect excuse to lick them clean—slowly, sensuously.

Her eyes darkened, her breath quickened, and her hand went limp as his tongue lapped along her fingers, and sucked them into his warm, wet mouth. "Mmm, *very* juicy and sweet," he agreed as he nibbled on one sensitive tip.

She visibly shivered, her nipples peaking against her bikini top, and not because she was cold. After retrieving her hand back, she abruptly stood and tossed the sunglasses still perched on her head onto the chaise. "Okay, I think I need to jump into the pool to cool off after that," she said, her voice filled with humor, probably to ward off the heated awareness that had settled between them. "Care to join me?"

He folded his hands over his stomach, preferring to watch rather than participate. "You go ahead. I'm good."

The view as she walked away was worth a million bucks. Her slim waist flared into nicely rounded hips, and she had an ass that was high and firm and connected to long, slender legs that prompted images of how they'd feel wrapped around him tight in the throes of passion. She could have easily posed for *Playboy* and made a fortune with that centerfold body, but he loved that she wasn't one to exploit herself, or her sensuality. But he had no doubt she'd give it all to one special man, and he wanted to be that lucky guy who laid final claim not only to her body, but her heart.

The possessive thought initially startled Will, but he couldn't deny that Ali still had a hold over him, that there were still feelings between them that could lead to something far more lasting than a weekend fling. But first he had to be honest with her, something he planned to do tonight.

She dove beneath the surface making a minimal splash, and swam the length in steady, even strokes. She did a few laps, then took the steps back out of the pool, rising like a gorgeous, tempting water nymph—blond hair slicked back, droplets falling off her body, her skin wet and gleaming, and tempting him to run his hands over all that sleek, slick flesh. Or his tongue. Oh, yeah, he liked that idea. A whole lot.

His private little fantasy made him grow hard and he shifted on his lounge chair for a more comfortable position. Hell, maybe he should have gone in for a cold dip, too.

Stopping next to his chaise, she squeezed the excess moisture from her hair, then grabbed her towel and took her time drying off. "That felt *really* good." She sighed like a woman who'd just indulged in some incredible sex.

He clenched his jaw. Jesus, she was *killing* him. She stood directly in front of him, putting Will at eye level with the crux of her thighs and the material that clung to that sweet spot hidden beneath her bikini bottoms. Desperately needing to focus on something less enticing, especially since they were out in public, he shifted his gaze higher. The pretty crystal belly ring she wore sparkled in the sunlight, catching his attention, and he reached out and touched the dangling bit of jewelry.

"I like your sunflower." Geez, even *that* sounded sexual.

"Thanks." Oblivious to where his mind had wandered, she laid her damp towel over her chair and sat back down, stretching out like a pagan goddess. "I pierced my navel in a small act of rebellion after my breakup, but I actually really like it. It reminds me that I need to make choices for me, and no one else."

She'd never struck him as the defiant type, but she'd obviously felt the need to exert independence after she found herself standing at the altar with no groom. Last night, she'd managed to skirt the issue of the painful details about what had happened the day of her wedding. But now, he took a chance and brought it up because he wanted to know what had gone wrong. How could any man have been foolish enough to walk away from a kind, caring and beautiful woman as Ali, who, to him, was the complete package?

"What happened, Ali?" he asked.

She didn't pretend to not know what he was referring to. She slipped her sunglasses back on, possibly to shield her expressive eyes from him as she looked his way. "Michael was a nice enough guy," she said, her tone slightly apprehensive, as if she really didn't want to talk about her past, but didn't want to keep it from him, either. "He's a partner at a big law firm in Chicago, and my parents instantly loved him. After five months of dating he asked me to marry him."

She gave a small shrug. "At the time, it seemed so easy to say yes. He told me I fit perfectly into his life, and I think that was part of the problem. I fit into his life on a professional level, but not a personal, intimate level. I was great at being the quiet, supportive girlfriend who accompanied him to dinners and work functions, who looked the part of an attorney's wife, but there was no real passion between us. I wasn't happy like a woman should be when she's about to marry the love of her life…because he *wasn't* the love of my life."

Will listened intently, though he remained quiet, letting her tell the story in her own way, in her own time.

"Michael was obviously having doubts, too, though we never really talked about it, which was another huge flaw in

our relationship. We just didn't *talk* the way a couple should."
Her hair had begun to dry in soft, loose curls, and she tucked
them back behind her ear. While her eyes were still shaded
from his view, there was no concealing the raw emotion in
her voice. "The day of this big, grand wedding, I was a mess,
and my mother assured me that it was all normal wedding
day jitters. But I knew she was wrong, that getting married
to Michael was wrong. Still I was so afraid of disappointing
everyone and causing a big scandal by calling off the marriage. Pretty stupid, huh?"

"Not at all," he said softly, refusing to judge Ali or the situation. "I'm sure it was a very difficult thing to go through."

She nodded, seemingly grateful that he understood. "About
a half hour before I was supposed to walk down the aisle,
Michael came to see me and told me he couldn't marry me.
He said he wasn't happy and he'd made a huge mistake. And
that easily, it was over."

"I'm sorry," he murmured, because it seemed the right
thing to say.

She shook her head. "He did the right thing. We both would
have been miserable in the long run. I mean, don't get me
wrong, his rejection hurt and the situation was humiliating.
People gossiped and speculated for months about what *I'd*
done to make Michael call off the wedding. I have to admit,
that part had been tough."

Will couldn't help but see the similarities between her
broken engagement, and the way he'd treated her back in
high school. He remembered the gossip that had run rampant throughout the school after he'd canceled their date, the
hurtful rumors that had put Ali in the spotlight, and not in a
good way. At the time, he honestly believed he'd been doing
her a favor, that he never really had a real shot with her any-
ways. Now, seeing the situation as an adult ten years later,
he knew better.

She reached out and picked up a slice of peach from the tray and took a bite. "As difficult as all that was with Michael, it made me realize that I can't settle. I want passion. And I deserve to be happy, no matter what choices I make. And every choice I've made since then has been for *me,* because it's what *I* want, and not because I think it's the right thing to do."

He heard the strength and determination in her voice, and smiled. "Are you happy now?"

Her gaze met his, her irises a bright green shot with threads of gold. "At this moment? *Very,*" she said meaningfully, her answer telling Will that she'd included him in her equation. "Though there's always room for a little more happiness in my life."

"And passion." He grinned wickedly.

"Yeah, that, too," she said, her voice dropping to a husky pitch.

Her phone beeped, and she picked it up to read the text message that just came through. "Looks like it's time for me to check in for my massage and facial."

She stood up and started gathering her things, but before she left, Will wanted to ask her something. It was ridiculous, but even now, ten years later, he felt a little nervous asking her out. "Ali, are you going to the reunion's dinner and dance tonight?"

She'd been bending over to grab her bag, tormenting him with another glimpse of her ass before she straightened and glanced at him, a tentative look in her eyes. "Depends on who is asking."

"I am." The sun shone behind her, and he had to squint to see her face. Her expression seemed a bit reserved. "Would you go with me?"

A slow smile curved her lips. "Are you asking me out on a date, Will Beckman?"

Oh, yeah, déjà vu. Those were the same words she'd spoken ten years ago, when he'd tried, albeit so very awkwardly, to invite her to the movies with him. "Yes, I am."

She thought for a too long moment, probably to make him suffer a bit. Then she finally let him off the hook. "I'd love to go to the dinner and dance with you. You can call my room later, number 641, and let me know when you'll be by to pick me up."

Looking *very* happy, Ali strolled off toward the hotel for her spa appointment.

Will watched her go, knowing that this time, there would be no standing her up, no rejection, no heartache, and absolutely no regrets. Because tonight, he was going to do everything he'd done wrong all those years ago, *right*.

# 5

RIGHT ON TIME, A KNOCK sounded on Ali's hotel room door. She did one last quick check of her reflection in the dresser mirror. For tonight's dinner and dance, she'd bought a slightly more close-fitting dress than she normally wore and she had to admit that the off-the-shoulder bodice and the formfitting material across her midsection did fabulous things for her figure, making her feel incredibly sexy. She was completely relaxed from her hot stone massage, and her skin and face glowed from all the extra pampering, too.

Slipping into her three-inch heels, she grabbed her clutch and headed for the door. When she opened it and saw Will standing on the other side looking devastatingly handsome in a classic black suit, she was completely awestruck by the gorgeous, confident man he'd become.

"Wow," he murmured, his dark blue gaze drinking her in, from her loose, blond curls all the way down to the tips of her one and only pair of black patent Louboutins. "You look incredible."

She flushed, feeling a bit giddy deep inside. "Thank you."

After last night and their time together this afternoon, there was a certain vibe in the air, one filled with all sorts of possibilities. Tonight she was going to enjoy everything about this night with Will—even if they were spending most of it with their classmates. For her, this was the date that should have been. When she walked into the dinner dance with Will, she had no doubt she'd be the envy of all the women there.

"Ready to go?" He held out his arm in a very sweet and romantic gesture.

"I am." Smiling, she looped her arm through his and they headed toward the elevators, looking very much like a couple.

"Did you enjoy your time at the spa?" he asked, his tone curious.

"Very much. It was quite a luxurious treat." She glanced at him, wondering how he'd spent the past few hours. "What did you do this afternoon? Anything fun or exciting?"

"I walked around and explored the resort." He grinned as he pushed the button for the elevator, which opened right away. Once they were inside, he continued. "Did you know that they even have a carnival here on-site, with arcade games and all sorts of rides?"

"I had no idea." But she wasn't surprised, considering that Celebrations catered to all kinds of reunions, including some that even involved kids. "This place has it all, doesn't it?"

"Pretty much." The elevator arrived on the ground floor, and Will led the way first across the lobby, then out a side door to a softly lit pathway.

Ali frowned, and tugged on his arm. "We're going the wrong way. Tonight's dinner is in the Festival ballroom, back in the hotel."

He stopped, but didn't turn around, just glanced down at her, his expression hopeful. "I planned something quieter and more intimate for dinner, for just the two of us. After that, we can make an appearance at the dance. Is that okay?"

"Absolutely." She was more than okay with being alone with Will, instead of being seated at a large round table where the conversation was loud and intrusive, with people she had no interest reminiscing with.

Happily now, she followed Will, until they came to a small, intimate outdoor atrium, filled with fragrant flowers and lush plants. A gazebo, strung with thousands of white twinkling lights, sat in the midst of it, and inside was set with a linen-draped table and chairs for their dinner.

Blown away by this very romantic setting, which Will must have arranged that afternoon, she climbed the stairs, grateful that he'd gently pressed a hand against the base of her spine to keep her steady. He held out a chair for her, and she sat down, recovering from her speechless surprise. "I think you've outdone yourself."

He settled in the seat across from her, looking very pleased with himself. "I had a lot to make up for."

She knew he was referring to their canceled date ten years ago, and the fallout after the fact, which made her appreciate even more all the thought he'd put into tonight to make this special. "This is going to be pretty hard to top as a first date."

He smiled at her. "I'd like to think it's going to be your *last* first date."

The implication was clear—not just with him, but with *anyone*. Wow. He was clearly staking a claim, noting that whatever this thing was between them, it was stronger than before and he wanted more.

Before she could reply, a male voice interrupted the moment.

"Good evening," the waiter said, holding an open bottle of wine in his hand as he came up the steps of the gazebo, then poured them each a glass of wine. "I'm Geoffrey, your personal waiter for this evening. Our chef has prepared a dinner of chateaubriand, with wild mushroom risotto and seared green beans. I'll be starting you off with a salad with a walnut pomegranate vinaigrette."

And so the evening's courses began. As they were served each dish, she and Will discussed anything and everything, from his company, to some of the more well-known clients she'd done graphic artwork for, as well as what they each enjoyed doing in their lives now. He even touched on why he was single after all these years, telling her that money and success had a way of skewing a woman's view of him. He hadn't found someone who was interested in *him*. And not what his wealth could provide. Because she knew him from way back, had *liked* him from the start, he trusted her, she realized, and that gave her a special place in his world aside from this very strong attraction.

They still had a lot in common, and it was clear to Ali that at the core, they were just ordinary people who enjoyed the simple things in life, as well as each other's company. Immensely. Throughout dinner, their conversation was easy and comfortable, marked with plenty of teasing and laughter, and by the end of the dessert she was feeling utterly content, in more ways than one.

Once the empty plates were cleared and they were alone once more, Will moved his chair so that he was sitting next to Ali. He was so close that he was able to grab her hand and hold it in his. Suddenly, his gaze turned serious, and she wondered what had prompted the unexpected change in him.

He cleared his throat, his gaze holding hers steadily. "There's something I've been wanting to tell you, about why things ended so badly between us in high school."

Ali was aware that he'd never given her a reason for the breakup. After his heartfelt apology, and spending the past two days with him, she'd simply chalked it all up to high school drama and teenage angst. "It's okay. It doesn't matter."

He exhaled a deep breath, but forged ahead, determined to have this discussion with her. "I'm glad to hear you say that, but I want this out in the open between us, because it matters to me."

She couldn't stem the flutter of worry that took flight in her stomach—she had no idea where this conversation was about to lead. But she wasn't about to deny him the chance to explain, if that's what he needed to do. "Okay."

He brushed his thumb over the knuckles of the hand he held, his warm touch chasing away the uneasy chill starting to take root inside her. "It's not a secret that I was a target for the bullies at school. One of the worst offenders was Tim Delgado."

She winced, because her own past with Tim had been tumultuous, too, for different reasons. "I know."

"After I asked you out, and you accepted, word spread around school pretty fast about the nerd who was dating the cheerleader. A few days later Tim and some of his football buddies cornered me after school and told me that you were *his* girl, and if I didn't break things off with you completely, I'd be very sorry."

"I wasn't his girl," she said, angry that Tim would make such a claim. He'd manipulated Will. And *her*. "I went to the prom with him and that was it." The prom, which had been a complete disaster because of Tim's obnoxious behavior, had been a few weeks before Will had asked her out, long after she'd ended things with Tim.

"That night, he made sexual advances toward me, and when I refused, he pushed the issue and told me I was just playing hard to get. He liked playing that game just fine because it made sex that much better." Just thinking about the incident made her sick all over again. "When he dropped me off at home, I told him we were done. For good."

"Well, he obviously believed differently." Will continued to caress her hand, as if touching her made it easier for him to spill this agonizing secret he'd kept to himself all these years. "At first I told Tim I wouldn't break things off with you, that he had no say in who I dated. Two days later, on that Friday afternoon when we were supposed to go out, he caught me alone again. But this time, he didn't just verbally threaten me. He physically assaulted me. And I was no match against a burly linebacker. One hit to the stomach, and I went down. He continued to kick me in the stomach until I was doubled over in pain and literally couldn't breathe." Will glanced away, but not before she saw the shame in his gaze. "He told me to expect much worse if I didn't call off the date, and I had no reason not to believe him. So, I called you and told you that I'd changed my mind, that I wasn't interested in you any longer."

Ali remembered that phone call verbatim, and how upset and confused she'd been that he'd just dumped her without an explanation. But now she knew, and her throat closed up with the pain and heartache of knowing what Will had suffered.

"Oh, God, Will." She placed her palm on his cheek and made him look her in the eyes again. "Why didn't you tell me the truth about what happened? Why didn't you report Tim to the school?"

He laughed, but the sound lacked any real humor. "I didn't tell *anyone* because I was mortified and humiliated. I didn't want to bring attention to what had happened to me, how I couldn't defend myself. I was already teased for being a computer nerd. This would have made things worse. And I couldn't bring myself to tell you the truth because you had the guts to actually say yes to the date. You took a chance on us despite what your friends thought, and I couldn't even stand up to Tim the way I should have."

She swallowed past the lump growing in her throat, because now it was her time to come clean. "I have something to confess, too."

His brows knitted into a frown, and he waited for her to go on.

"I was so excited when you asked me out, but I suffered a lot of backlash from my friends because of it," she said, releasing her own painful secret. "And when you called off the date, while I was hurt and upset, a very small part of me was relieved. I wouldn't be subjected to any more gossip and whispers behind my back. It was so selfish and stupid, and I'm so sorry, for all of it."

"I get it, Ali. And I understand." His expression gentled, and he leaned forward and pressed his forehead to hers. "God, being a teenager *sucks*. It's not easy for anyone, is it? The nerd *or* the cheerleader."

The amusing note to his voice made her smile, and she knew everything was going to be okay between the two of them. "I guess not. As teenagers, we all have our issues to deal with. I'm just glad you came to the reunion, that you and I had the chance to finally get everything out in the open and start again. As adults who don't care what other people think or say."

"Agreed." He leaned even closer and touched his lips to hers in a soft, reverent kiss filled with unending promise before pulling back just a bit, his eyes now glimmering with affection, all for her. "There's still one part left to our evening. What do you say you and I head into the reunion for a bit of dancing?"

She thought about suggesting they skip the dance altogether for more sensual pursuits, but there was a part of her that wanted to make up for the past. She was going to walk into that ballroom with Will on her arm to show everyone that the cheerleader and the nerd were an item. She was damned proud of it.

Liking that idea, she placed her hand in his and stood. "With you, absolutely."

HAND IN HAND, WILL WALKED with Ali back into the hotel lobby and down a wide hallway that led to the Festival ballroom where the class of 2002 was in the midst of enjoying the evening's gala. As they stepped inside the room, he realized that while dinner was over for the guests, they were now watching a slide show of old high school pictures and topics that had been specific to the year they'd graduated. World events flashed on the screen, along with the top grossing movies, sports trivia and other fun and interesting subjects from that time period.

Quietly, he sat down with Ali in the very back of the room, so that they, too, could watch the display. Songs from 2002 accompanied the presentation, and the one currently playing was Kylie Minogue's "Can't Get You Out of My Head."

Ali leaned in close and cupped her hand around her mouth to whisper in his ear. "When you were tutoring me, that was my song for you. I played it on my iPod constantly."

He grinned, and they went back to viewing the slide show. Other familiar songs followed, such as No Doubt's "Underneath It All" and ended on Kelly Clarkson's "A Moment Like This." When the lights went back on, the DJ announced that the dance floor was open and that everyone should get their groove on.

The only person Will wanted to get his groove on with was Ali. They'd come to the function to dance, but after a few songs they'd be out of there. He intended to spend the rest of the night alone with her, just the two of them. After all, they had a lot of lost time to make up for.

Keeping their fingers entwined, he guided her toward the dance floor, feeling like the luckiest man on earth. He'd been given a second chance with the woman by his side. Their conversation out in the gazebo had changed everything between them, had brought them closer. And it closed a chapter in their lives that no longer mattered. Life was good.

Alumni watched and stared as they worked their way around the tables, his hold on Ali possessive enough to let everyone know she was his. It didn't take long for people to start talking, taking note of the fact that they were now clearly a couple.

Reaching the dance floor, he spun her around in his arms in rhythm to the fast tune currently playing. "A few dances, and then you're *mine* for the rest of the night," Will growled against her ear, uncaring of how aggressive he sounded.

She didn't seem to mind. She flashed him a flirtatiously sexy smile. "Oh, I'm counting on it." Then she slipped back out of his grasp and let the upbeat music dictate her very sensual dance moves.

Oh, yeah, it was going to be a *very* good night, Will thought.

Three fast songs finally segued into a slow melody, and Will didn't hesitate to pull Ali right back into his embrace. The dance floor was fairly crowded, and the other couples around them joined in, enjoying a little close time with their significant others.

Ali's body aligned perfectly with his. As he looked into her flushed, smiling face, he couldn't remember ever wanting a woman as much as he desired her. "Will you come up to my room with me tonight?" It was a straightforward question, leaving no doubts to what, exactly, he meant. He wanted her in his room and in his bed.

"I'd like that," she murmured, her green eyes shining with the same sensual kind of need that thrummed though his veins. "*Very* much."

His gaze dropped to her parted lips, and it took a Herculean effort not to kiss her in front of everyone. It was one thing to let their classmates know they were a couple, but quite another to make out like out-of-control teenagers in front of them. "As soon as this song is over, we'll go, okay?"

She feigned a pout, her plump bottom lip tempting him even more. "You're going to make me wait that long?" she teased.

She obviously didn't know the restraint it took for him to be a gentleman, because he was so damn close to hauling her over his shoulder and walking out of the ballroom with her, caveman-style. Yeah, that would set tongues wagging, for sure. "It'll be worth the wait. I promise."

"Hey, I've been looking for you, Ali," a too-familiar voice drawled from behind Will, putting him on full alert.

Tim had managed to make his way through the crowd and stood next to them. Ali's entire body tensed, and her expression filled with dread. It was clear that Tim had been drinking. And the guy never had a problem making a scene or drawing attention to himself, even when he was sober.

Will knew that whatever was about to happen wasn't going to be good—even the couples slow dancing next to them started moving away, giving them a wider berth. And while Will's first instinct was to flatten the guy, he decided to keep his temper in check for the time being.

Tim ignored Will and gave Ali a grin that was more like a crude leer. "How 'bout a dance, for old time's sake?"

More politely than Tim deserved, Ali looked at him and said, "No, thanks."

"Aww, come on, Ali," Tim said, his voice turning into a taunting sneer. "You know you want to."

"No, I really don't." She glared at Tim, her jaw clenched in irritation. "Just go. You're making a fool of yourself."

He made a snorting sound, like a half-assed laugh. "Jeez, you don't have to be such a bitch about it."

That was it. Will had had enough. He released Ali and faced his nemesis. "Back off, Tim," he said, his voice vibrating with barely suppressed anger. "Ali said *no*."

Tim turned his narrowed gaze on Will and puffed out his

chest, like a cocky rooster getting ready for a fight. "Back off? Really?" He stepped closer, invading Will's personal space. "And what are you going to do if I don't?"

Will's hands curled into fists as his sides as he and Tim locked gazes. Will was not a fighter, but those memories of how Tim had mercilessly beat the crap out of him were strong and overwhelming, making him itch to give a little payback. He certainly wasn't afraid of Tim any longer, but neither was he one to instigate a physical assault, either.

"Yeah, that's what I thought. You've got nothing," Tim said, as if he'd won that round. "You might have a billion dollars to your name, but you still don't have the guts to throw a punch, do you, nerd?"

Will said nothing, but as he glanced around at the people who were watching the encounter unfold, he realized that most everyone was looking at Tim with disappointment and pity. Tim, once a golden linebacker with a promising future, was nothing more than a washed-up alcoholic football player who still felt the need to put down others in order to build up his own self-esteem. It was pathetic, really.

"Tim, *stop it,*" Ali said, her voice low and furious.

"Stop it?" Tim mocked, his expression turning mean. "Are you kidding me? I'm just getting started. In fact, I think you and I ought to have a prom night do-over." He grabbed Ali's arm and tugged her closer. "And maybe this time you won't be so uptight about putting out. Or are you just putting out for *him?*"

Livid that Tim would dare to even touch Ali, Will didn't think, just reacted. His fist flew out, slamming into Tim's jaw and snapping his head back. The strength and momentum behind the punch sent the other man stumbling backward and flat on his ass. The crowd gasped in shock and awe, but no one bothered to help Tim up. The man lay prone, trying to gather his bearings.

"He's had that coming to him for a long time," Will heard someone around him say.

"Man, that was priceless," another person said, their tone gleeful. "This is the best reunion *ever*."

Will stepped up to where Tim was still on the ground and pointed a harsh finger at him. "You touch Ali again, Delgado, and I personally guarantee you'll regret it."

Will turned back to Ali, who was staring wide-eyed at him in bewildered admiration, of all things. Adrenaline rushed through his veins, and he had to admit he was feeling like quite the badass at the moment.

"Let's get the hell out of here," he said, grabbing Ali's hand. He started toward the entrance and their classmates parted the way for them, issuing verbal support and accolades for giving the high school bully exactly what he deserved.

Once they were inside the elevator, Will leaned against the wall and Ali pressed her body flush to the length of his, tilting her smiling, radiant face up to his.

"Oh, my God, you hit him," she said, laughing joyously as her hands rubbed against his chest. "I can't believe you hit him."

Will grinned as he wrapped one arm around her waist and shook the sting out of the hand that had punched Tim. "Not one of my finer moments, but *nobody* touches you like that and gets away with it."

The adoration in her eyes made him feel like a superhero. "Seeing you deck Tim on my behalf… Oh, wow, that was so *hot*." She buried her face in his neck and started kissing his throat. "Would it shock you if I told you that seeing you get all barbaric and aggressive turned me on?"

Heat shot straight to Will's groin, hardening him in a flash. "Yeah, well, how's *this* for barbaric?" he teased, and gave in to the urge to heft her over his shoulder just as the elevator doors opened on his floor.

He carried her down to his room, her bright, infectious squeals and giggles echoing throughout the hallway. She might be laughing now, but by the time he was done with her, the only thing he'd be hearing would be moans of pleasure.

# 6

AS SOON AS THEY WERE INSIDE Will's hotel room, he gently set Ali on her feet. She barely had a moment to gain her equilibrium after being carried upside down before he backed her against the nearest wall and kissed her like a starving man. She kissed him back with just as much greed. His hands eagerly worked the zipper at the back of her dress while she shoved his coat off and attacked the buttons on his shirt, nearly tearing them off in her haste to get him naked.

Once the material was unfastened, he shrugged out of the garment, enabling her to finally touch him. She splayed her hands on his bare chest, reveling in the heat of his skin and the firm muscles bunching beneath her palms. She rubbed her thumbs over his nipples and he groaned into their still-fused mouths.

He finally managed to completely unzip her dress, and the loosened fabric slithered down the length of her body and pooled around her feet, leaving her in just her bra, panties and designer heels. She skimmed her fingers down his flat stomach to the waistband of his slacks, then lower, caressing the thick length of his erection through his pants before fumbling with the opening to his trousers.

To her surprise, he grasped her wrists and pulled her hands

away. Breaking their kiss, he pulled back slightly to look at her, his eyes burning with lust and need. "Not yet, Ali," he said, his tone low and rough. "I want you so damn badly that if you so much as touch me, I'm done. And there's way too much I want to do to you first."

Seeing Will so close to losing control, a delicious shiver of anticipation coursed through Ali. Knowing they had all night together, that she'd get her chance to have her way with him later, she gladly indulged his request. "I'm all yours."

He released her hands, and she let them fall back to her sides. He stood a small step back, just enough so that he could look his fill of her. He ran a finger from her collarbone down to the swells of her breasts above the cups of her pale pink satin-and-lace bra. With a deliberate slowness that made her a little bit crazy, he traced the strap back up to her shoulder, then pulled both of them down her arms, all the way to her elbows, until the pretty piece of lingerie peeled away to reveal her full breasts to his worshipful gaze.

"So gorgeous," he said, his tone reverent.

She bit her bottom lip. Her breasts were large, but still firm and high, and he pressed his palms to both of the aching mounds, caressing and squeezing the plump flesh. She made a small, wordless approving noise in the back of her throat as he gently pinched her sensitive nipples. And when he dipped his head and pulled a taut peak into his mouth and sucked her deep, she gasped and plunged all ten of her fingers into his hair for something to hold on to.

His tongue licked and laved, teased and tormented, and the scrape of his teeth added another dimension of pleasure that shot liquid heat straight between her thighs. One of his hands slid down her stomach, stopped briefly to play with her belly ring, then continued south. Finding the waistband of her panties, he slipped his fingers beneath the elastic edge and in the next instant he was touching her exactly where she needed him the most.

Shuddering against him, she spread her legs wider, giving him every bit of access as he explored her delicate folds with seductive caresses and deep, penetrating strokes that pushed her straight toward the promise of a sweet, hot release. Coupled with the wet, suctioning warmth of his mouth on her breast, and she was so done. Clutching his hair in her fists, she gave herself over to the experience, moaning as the intense need took her and her climax rolled through her in a huge, pulsating wave of pure ecstasy that left every part of her body quivering in the aftermath.

His mouth found hers again and he kissed her deeply, hungrily. Then he swept her up in his arms and carried her to the big king-size bed, placing her in the middle. As she looked up at him, waiting for him to get undressed and join her, she saw a moment of clarity darken his eyes.

"Condom," he said gruffly. "I'll be right back."

Will hadn't come to the reunion expecting to have sex, but lucky for him, he did have a few spare condoms in his shaving bag. He grabbed them quickly from the bathroom and returned to find that Ali had removed her bra, panties and shoes, and now lay against the cool sheets and fluffy pillows, gloriously, breathtakingly naked, except for the sunflower jewel glittering so very invitingly in her navel. His mouth went dry as dust.

Then she gave him a come-hither smile, crooked her finger seductively at him, and he didn't hesitate a moment longer. In record time he had the rest of his clothes stripped off and protection on. Starting at the foot of the bed, he moved toward her, skimming his hands up her calves. When he reached her knees, he pushed her legs wide apart and dipped his head to kiss and nibble his way up the inside of her thighs, until he reached the heart of her. Settling in, he draped her legs over his shoulders, tilting her even closer to his hungry mouth.

A moan of anticipation escaped her. Her hands fisted in the sheets, and when he finally slid his tongue between the lips of her sex and swirled it around her clit, she went wild, lifting her hips off the bed for more pressure, more friction. Wetting his finger in her body's slick moisture, he pushed it into her, then another, stroking slowly, deeply, making her gasp and writhe and finally beg with the need to come again.

He gave her the orgasm she craved, reveling in the tight grip of her body around his fingers and her soft, ragged cries of rapture as she rode the surging swell of her climax. Desperately wanting to share in the moment, to be a part of her pleasure before it completely ebbed, he moved over her, tangling his fingers in her hair and pulling her head back to kiss her with possessive heat and a need so intense it superseded anything he'd ever felt before. And he knew that this woman, that Ali, was the reason.

She wrapped her legs around his hips, urging him to take her, and he did, driving into her lush body with a hard, demanding thrust that had him sliding all the way home. She was warm and pliant and still pulsing from her powerful orgasm, and it took him a moment to gain control again before he could move inside her without things ending before they really had the chance to begin.

He lifted his mouth from hers, his harsh breathing fanning against her cheek as he slowly withdrew, then just as gradually pushed back inside her. He did it again, and again, controlling every tantalizing thrust, every deliberate move, while building sensation upon sensation. Her fingers dug into the taut muscles along his back, and her hips circled against his in a slow, provocative mating dance.

"Will," she whispered, arching into him, clearly seeking a harder, faster pace.

He heard the impatience in her voice, but wasn't ready to pick up his stride just yet. He wanted this first time to be memorable and perfect. He nuzzled and kissed her neck, then dragged his mouth up to the lobe of her ear. "What do you feel, Ali?"

"You," she moaned as he filled her up again. "Deep inside me."

*Oh, yeah.* She squeezed him from within, holding on to his cock so tightly he felt wrapped in a glove of the softest, smoothest velvet. Raising his head to look at her flushed face, he met and held her desire infused gaze as he stretched into her once more, grinding just a bit harder, a bit deeper than before, wringing a startled gasp from her lips. "What else do you feel?"

She smiled at him then, leaving no doubt in Will's mind that she was experiencing the same things he was. "Passion," she said as her hands traveled down the slope of his back to his buttocks, which she grabbed to pull him tighter against her. "So. Much. Passion."

Now he was ready to finish, to give them both what they wanted. He crushed his mouth to hers and took her the way he'd been dying to…steadily, relentlessly, without an ounce of restraint holding him back. He plunged harder, faster and then he was coming, groaning raggedly against her lips as she contracted around him, milking the last of his orgasm and leaving him completely and thoroughly spent.

FEELING THE SUN STREAMING through the window, Ali rolled onto her back and stretched her naked body beneath the covers, her muscles delightfully sore after a night spent making love with Will. Numerous times and numerous ways. Lord, the man had been insatiable and so incredibly inventive.

Smiling to herself, she opened her eyes and turned her head on her pillow to find that she was completely alone in bed. Another glance toward the open bathroom door confirmed that Will wasn't in the hotel room with her. There wasn't a note anywhere from what she could see, causing a sense of dread to settle in the pit of her stomach.

She closed her eyes and swallowed hard. Unbidden, the past and the present collided in her mind, sending her first thoughts in the direction of how it felt to be rejected, to put her heart out there only to have those emotions not be reciprocated. And oh, Lord, she'd definitely let her emotions run rampant last night. Will was exactly the kind of man she could fall in love with—if she wasn't already halfway there. But there was no telling what last night had meant to *him*.

Unfortunately, old fears died hard, and it was all she could do not to let her doubts overwhelm her. What she needed to do was get up, get dressed and wait for Will to return and go from there.

She started to move, but before she had the chance to even toss back the comforter, the door opened and Will walked inside, carrying two paper cups. Since she was still naked, she remained exactly where she was.

"Morning," he greeted her cheerfully.

"Morning," she replied a bit more quietly.

"Coffee is a necessity for me in the morning," he said, explaining his absence as he set the cups on the table in the corner. "You were sleeping so soundly, I didn't want to wake you."

She was relieved that he'd returned, that he'd only left for coffee, but that meant nothing in terms of their future together.

He'd changed into a pair of faded jeans and plain T-shirt for his quick errand. He started toward her side of the bed, and it was really no fair that he looked so damned gorgeous after a night of debauchery with his tousled hair, shadowed jaw and bright blue eyes while she probably looked hideously disheveled.

Suddenly feeling self-conscious, she tugged the sheet higher on her chest and attempted to run her fingers through her wild curls, wincing as she hit a series of tangles, confirming her worst fears.

He sat down on the mattress right beside her. "You look beautiful," he said huskily, as if reading her mind, then leaned down to kiss her lips. "Passion agrees with you, sweetheart."

Her face bloomed with warmth at his compliment. Relaxing, she touched her fingers to his stubbled cheek, enjoying the slight scrape against her skin and thinking about how it would feel rubbing against her breasts, or between her thighs. "There certainly was a lot of that happening last night," she agreed.

His wicked grin slowly faded away, and his expression turned more pensive. "It's the last day of the reunion, and I think we need to talk about us."

"Okay." Her hand fell away from his jaw and a familiar twinge of uneasiness settled in her belly at his serious tone. For all they'd shared over the past few days, there had been no discussion about the two of them beyond the weekend. And even though they both lived in Chicago, assuming that Will wanted anything more than just a fling was awfully presumptuous of her.

He frowned at her. "You went there, didn't you?"

She blinked at him, startled by the question. "Went where?" But she knew exactly what he was referring to, because her first line of defense in this kind of situation was to kick up walls to protect her from the potential hurt of rejection.

"Ali, I don't want to end things," he said gently, sincerely—the way the Will she knew him to be would do. "For me, this is just the beginning of something really great and lasting. And…oh, hell, I'm falling for you, big-time."

He shocked her again, and while she was momentarily speechless, her heart was doing a big happy dance.

When she didn't immediately reply, it was his turn to look a bit nervous. "Unless you feel differently?"

"No. No, of course not!" She laughed, shaking her head at their miscommunication, feeling a huge wave of delight wash over her. "I feel the same way about you. I was so infatuated with you in high school, and now, well…I want this, and I want *you*."

He exhaled a deep breath, his relief evident. "In that case, I have something very special for you."

He left the bed and went to his suitcase. After pulling out a small black velvet-lined box, he returned to Ali, and she sat up on the mattress, curious to know what was in the jewelry box.

He met her gaze, grinning a bit wickedly. "So, at the end of our senior year, you were voted the Girl Most Likely to Become a Playboy Bunny."

"Obviously, that didn't happen," she said, and laughed.

His fingers played with the box in his hand. "And we both know that Tim got all his friends to vote me the Guy Most Likely to Date a Playboy Bunny, NOT, because you and I weren't ever going to be an item. Not in high school, anyway."

"And now?" she asked, knowing things had changed in a big way.

"Well, now, I'm one helluva lucky man, because I'm dating that Playboy Bunny," he said with a wicked grin. "And I want everyone to know it."

He opened the box, and what she saw made her breath catch at first, then she laughed out loud because the necklace he'd bought for her was perfect and priceless. At the end of a silver chain was a small pendant of the Playboy rabbit logo, encrusted in diamonds. Judging by the name of the jewelers inscribed inside the box, there was no doubt in Ali's mind that those sparkling gems were the real deal. The significance of the necklace wasn't lost on her, and spoke of Will's feelings for her back then, and now.

With her heart racing in her chest, she lifted an amused brow at Will. "You were a little confident in buying this, don't you think?" she asked cheekily.

"Not confident, but very hopeful." He took the necklace out and held it up for her. "Will you wear it?"

"Oh, yeah. I love it and what it means. It's our own personal, private joke." She lifted her hair off her neck and let him secure the chain for her. When he was done, the pendant nestled just below the hallow of her throat. "I can't wait for everyone at the reunion brunch today to see it and know that *you* got lucky, in more ways than one." She waggled her brows at him.

He chuckled and made quick work of removing his clothes, then pulled the covers away from her body and gently tumbled her back down to the bed, his already aroused body nestling into hers in all the right places. "Well, *you're* about to get lucky, Ali Seaver."

"We'll be late for brunch." The protest had no backing to it, not when he was already pushing inside her and she was melting around him, moaning with the pleasure to come.

He arched against her, high and hard, making her gasp as he filled her body, heart and soul. "Imagine the gossip we'll start. You all glowing from recent sex, wearing a Playboy pendant around your neck."

She smiled, for once not minding that she'd be the center of speculation. Not when it meant she'd landed the greatest guy ever.

\* \* \* \* \*

# JULIE LETO

A MOMENT LIKE THIS

To Janelle and Leslie.

# _1_

_Ten years ago..._
_St. Aloysius High School_

"YOU'RE USING YOUR TONGUE wrong."

Erica Holt sat up straighter and adjusted her headphones. The computerized French instructor she'd been practicing with for the past hour spoke again, this time making no further reference to Erica's tongue. But wait...how could the disembodied voice know if Erica was using her mouth correctly? The school's Listening Lab computer program wasn't _that_ interactive.

When she felt a tap on her shoulder, she nearly jumped out of her skin.

"You're using your tongue wrong," the guy standing behind her repeated.

Erica blinked, confused. No one was supposed to be in the school after four-thirty, least of all Scott Ripley. She was only there because she had a special pass from the headmaster. But of all the people who might have stumbled into the classroom specifically equipped for foreign language students to practice their pronunciations, she never expected to see him.

Did he even go to class?

The Class of 2002's most notorious bad boy grabbed one of the St. Aloysius navy blue chairs and twirled it backward to sit. He was still talking to her—something she was pretty sure he'd never done in the four years they'd been in school together—but she couldn't hear him because the female voice in her headphones was insisting she repeat something about taking a shower.

Or maybe she was talking about bedtime. Erica wasn't sure.

She yanked off the headgear, taking with it the dark gold uniform headband she'd worn all day. Her hair was probably a mess. Not that it mattered. This was Rip Ripley. Her physical appearance made no difference to him. He didn't waste his time with girls who didn't put out…and if there was one thing Erica was known for in the hallowed halls of St. Aloysius, it was her sterling reputation.

"You're not supposed to be in here," she said.

"And you're not supposed to pronounce your *R*s as if you've never been kissed."

She shoved the headphones back on her head and turned back to her computer. She wasn't going to let Rip be such a… such a guy…around her. Despite attending the same small private school for going on four years, they'd never exchanged more than a few words. Not even when his aunt and uncle—his guardians since his parents weren't around for reasons that had spawned some of the most outrageous rumors ever spread around Chicago's Oak Park neighborhood—had her family over to their estate for parties or fundraisers.

By unspoken agreement, they ignored each other. She was, by nature, a very friendly girl. She liked socializing and didn't really know anyone at St. Aloysius she hadn't chatted with at one point or another. Even freshmen.

Except for Rip.

She decided not to change the rules now. Not when she had

an oral French exam tomorrow and she was so close to failing. Only a promise to secure her teacher an invitation to an exclusive Matisse showing at the Art Institute had convinced him not to call her parents. But the event was in three weeks and her mom and dad would be there. She'd bought herself twenty-one short days to turn her low D into at least a B, or she'd be grounded for the rest of the semester.

When Rip yanked her headphones off again, she squealed, not so much in surprise, but in frustration.

"What do you think you're doing?"

"Trying to talk to you," he answered. "You're being rude."

"I'm being rude? You're the one who snuck in here uninvited. It's after four-thirty. No students are supposed to be in the school unless under the direct supervision of a coach, faculty member or approved staff."

"Wow," he said, dropping back down onto his seat. His raven-dark hair swung over one eye, emphasizing the intense blue of the one still locked on her. "Do you purposefully memorize all the school rules or do you just have one of those photographic memories so you can't help it?"

She pressed her lips together tightly. "I'm student council president. It's my job to know all the rules."

"Ah," he said, leaning back so that his chair was balanced precariously on the chair's hind legs. "But is it your job to enforce them?"

"No."

"Then lighten up, Holt. I'm not here to destroy school property. Well, not now that I know you're here."

"What does that mean?"

His mouth crooked up at the corner into a half grin that made Erica understand why just about every girl in school was willing to shimmy out of her panties for him—and most of them had, if the rumors proved true.

"It means this is your lucky day," he said. "You averted

the brilliant plan I had for, um, updating the Listening Lab computers so they repeated a series of translated limericks. As a reward, you get a free French lesson."

"You don't speak French," she sniped, then before he could counter her claim, she amended, "And *voulez-vous coucher avec moi ce soir* doesn't count."

He combed his hair back, his blue eyes wide for a split second before he burst into laughter. "Do you even know what that means? Or what it would mean if you said it right?"

Heat rose up from deep in Erica's belly and shot straight to the apples of her cheeks. She'd made the stupid mistake of taking French 1 in her freshman year and putting off French 2 until she was a senior, but she'd seen *Moulin Rouge!*

Six times.

"Yes, I know what it means. I figured it was the one French phrase you would know. Intimately."

She arched a brow, just to make sure he understood that she was fully informed about his reputation as a player. From the way he chuckled, he clearly got the message.

But when he grabbed her hand and tugged her toward him, she nearly lost her breath. His eyes locked with hers, and then he spoke in perfectly accented French that would have made her teacher weep. She only picked up a few words. The ones she was pretty much sure meant things like *hidden, secret* and *forbidden.*

"I could help you," he offered.

It took a split second for Erica's brain to register that he'd switched back to English.

She pulled out of his grasp. "How do you speak so fluently?"

He shrugged. "I have an ear for languages. Besides, Monsieur Bernard doesn't take it so seriously when I show up a few minutes late for his class, so I actually go most of the time. I'm taking Advanced Conversational French 4."

"We don't have that course here," Erica said. She not only knew the student handbook back to front, she knew the course offerings.

"It's special study designed to ensure I show up for at least one class on a regular basis. And it gives me one more qualification for being your tutor."

"What's the other qualification?" she asked.

His gaze drifted to her mouth and when he licked his lips, she remembered what he'd said when he first spoke to her—about her using her tongue wrong. But despite the electric thrill that danced through her bloodstream unbidden and unappreciated, Erica knew better than to go down that road with Rip Ripley.

She liked her good reputation. She banked on it. A girl could get far in life when people always expected her to do the right thing.

She dropped the headphones into the bin. "No, thanks."

"Why not?"

"Oh, I don't know, because you don't usually speak to me, much less offer to teach me…"

To teach her…what? French? Or French kissing?

The prospect shot a second shiver through her system—one she'd deny until the day she died.

"You don't exactly talk to me, either," he countered.

"I talk to everyone," she said. It was a point of pride for her. She'd even made small talk with the people she didn't like, if the situation required it. Her real estate mogul father and socialite mother had always taught her to keep her friends close and her enemies closer.

Problem was, Rip was neither friend nor foe. He existed in her universe, but only on the fringes. They saw each other. She included him in collective "hellos" whenever she passed him hanging out with his buddies in the hall, but otherwise, each pretty much pretended the other didn't exist.

"Yes, I know. You are the perfect little politician, wrapping everyone in this school around your efficient little finger so they'll do your bidding on the prom committee or during food drives without complaint. Hey, I'm not judging," he said when she opened her mouth to object. "I'm impressed. You'd think you'd have a few haters somewhere, but I've never found any."

She arched a brow. "You were looking?"

He grinned, eliciting another simmering ripple through her body. "Not with as much energy as I put into figuring out how to reprogram the bell system so it lets us out a minute earlier every two days, but I keep my ear to the ground."

Erica shook her head, making a mental note to suggest that the headmaster have the bell system rechecked while she marveled at the fact that Rip Ripley thought about her enough to try and ferret out if she had any closeted enemies.

"And what have you discovered?"

He clucked his tongue as if wildly disappointed. "You're kind of boring."

"Compared to you, Jack Black is boring."

"So you listen to gossip about me, too? Sweet."

"A girl would have to be deaf not to hear gossip about you. I used to think you started half of the rumors yourself."

"And now?"

She thrust her hands onto her hips. "Now I think you take a lot of pleasure in making sure everything said about you is true."

He patted himself on the back. "Someone has to liven things up in this mausoleum. Look, as you so generously pointed out, I'm not exactly supposed to be hanging around here after hours. I may or may not have been warned by the headmaster that if he caught me breaking yet another of this prison's stupid rules, I'd be assigned to lunch duty. And while I'm pretty sure I can figure out a way to rock a hairnet, I'd rather not cut into my social hour with duties best left to the lunch ladies. Do you want my help or not?"

"I don't understand why you're offering."

"Neither do I, but it's real and it's your call. No one has to know that you're letting the big, bad Rip Ripley into your bedroom at night."

She scowled, not angry that he'd make such a suggestion, but that her belly would flip-flop a little at the thought. "Neutral location. Somewhere no one will see us. I don't need anyone thinking we're, you know, together, or anything."

"No, you definitely don't want anyone to think that. Should we work out a secret code to communicate with or will exchanging cell phone numbers be enough?"

Erica took a deep breath. In her seventeen short years, she'd learned that making the right choice in difficult situations wasn't all that hard. She just thought about what her father would do, or her mother, and she'd never been disappointed in the outcome.

But she couldn't rely on her parents for guidance this time. If they knew about her failing grade, they'd yank her straight out of her extracurricular activities. If she went to her teacher for more help than access to the Listening Lab, he might break his promise not to contact her parents until progress reports. She couldn't even access her savings account to pay for a proper tutor without alerting her family—and if she asked any of her other friends for help, they'd gossip about how St. Aloysius's "golden girl" was flunking French 2.

She had no option but trust the one guy in school who had a reason to keep her secret. If anyone found out that Rip Ripley was hanging out with Erica Holt, his bad boy rep would be ruined for good.

"Okay," she agreed.

"Okay," he repeated, his eyes flashing with an emotion

Erica couldn't identify for sure—but if she hadn't known better, she might have thought it was…anticipation.

*Present day*

SCOTT RIPLEY TUGGED his duffel out of his saddlebag, grunting at the weight. He should have left some of his crap at his aunt and uncle's house, where he'd stopped right after hitting town, but as he'd shown up in the middle of their bridge club, he'd opted to keep his visit short.

He had, however, promised to return for Sunday dinner. The prospect yanked a reluctant smile out of him. For years, he'd hated everything about his teen years—including the family that had taken him in after his father's arrest and his mother's overdose. He'd certainly made himself the bane of his aunt and uncle's existence, though he always stopped short of anything too serious—just enough to make him a serious pain in the ass and cost his uncle a fortune.

The man had spent hundreds—no, thousands—paying off business owners and school officials so that Rip's infractions didn't permanently scar his future. Now he was back in town with his proverbial hat in his hand, not to collect cover-up money, but to find funding for his foundation's newest program. He wasn't about to ask his uncle for a dime, but his wealthy classmates were another story.

In retrospect, high school hadn't been a total waste of time. He'd learned some things, made some friends. He hadn't been anxious to attend his reunion, but he'd make the best of it—a prospect that brightened when he heard the rumble of a well-made American hog coming up behind him.

So far, his was the only bike parked in the motorcycle lot of the Celebrations Resort. The closer the Harley got, the louder his blood pounded in his ears. For those formative teenage years, hopping onto the back of his ride and tearing through the neighborhoods of suburban Chicago on his way to meaner, more familiar streets had been the only thing that had saved his sanity. He loved the machines with a passion that skirted perilously close to obsession.

The hungry growl of the approaching Twin Cam 103™ engine was only foreplay. When he caught sight of the rider—a wet dream from the cut of her boots to the curves of her body—his prospects for the weekend ratcheted up to fantasy fulfillment.

She rolled to a stop in front of him, but didn't power down.

"Get on," she said.

The undeniably sultry, unmistakably feminine voice was barely audible over the engine, but even with her face shield down on her helmet, he knew she was hot. Clue one? Glossy red lips. Clue two? Flawless skin on her jaw, neck and cleavage. Clue three? The confident way she sat on her Harley-Davidson Softail Deluxe.

Oh, yeah. Hot as hell.

"Do I know you?" he asked, lowering his sunglasses.

"Not as well as you should," she replied, turning her helmeted head toward the tight space behind her. "But if you get on, you can change that."

He put his glasses back on. Things like this didn't happen to him every day—but he couldn't say it hadn't happened before. But this wasn't the Greased Handlebar out in Bakersfield or Sam's Slaughterhouse on the South Side. This was a five-star resort and this woman, despite the leather and denim gift wrap, was no ordinary back warmer.

At first glance, she looked entirely suited for the sleek machine between her legs. Her denim jeans were ripped at strategic intervals just beneath her knee and at midthigh. Her leather vest clung to curves that filled the supple hide with just the right amount of feminine flesh. And her boots—

black-heeled and scuffed—could kick a man squarely in his family jewels the second he got out of line.

"As enticing as your offer is, I don't ride with bikers I don't know," he replied.

"Who says you don't know me?"

Rip narrowed his gaze, wondering who this vixen could possibly be. In the ten years since he'd fulfilled his classmates' senior superlative by being the "Guy Most Likely to Ride out of Town on a Harley"—an award they'd created just for him when a drug-dealing classmate had beat him to "Mostly Likely to Spend Time in Prison"—he'd never once imagined that any of the debutantes from St. Aloysius High School would use their trust funds to buy a hog.

But people changed. If this chick knew him—and he was certain she did—somewhere underneath the tanned and dyed cowhide of her vest and ripped-up jeans was a prep school sweetheart in new, improved packaging.

The question was, which one?

"What are you afraid of?" she asked, curling her hands and revving her engines, making it harder to ignore her challenge—or identify her voice.

"The only thing I'm afraid of is you mishandling that machine," he replied.

Her crimson lips curled into a cocky grin. "Trust me, Rip. I can handle a hell of a lot more than you can imagine."

Rip stuffed his duffel into the saddlebag and locked his bike.

As he strapped on his helmet, she wiggled a little farther up the leather seat, drawing his eyes to her sweet little backside. He tried to imagine the curve of her ass in the pleated plaid of St. Aloysius High School's school uniform, but why go back to the past when the present was so much better? Though he'd spent a good portion of his school days concentrating on the sassy swing of his schoolmates' backsides rather than his books, he hadn't memorized them. Like the elements on the periodic table, there were just too many to remember. But this one felt pert and tight against his inner thighs and her waist barely required one arm to wrap around.

"Where're we going?" he asked as she eased the bike around a curve that led to the parking lot exit.

"Old haunt," she shouted before the fully throttled engine drowned out any possibility for further conversation.

She navigated the streets with ease, merging onto the highway without hesitation or fear, passing cars when she needed to, but never remaining well within the speed limits and road rules. A beautiful woman who could tame a Harley was a woman to be admired. Well, he had to assume she was beautiful. Her body was certainly smoking. Coupled with gorgeous lips and luscious dark hair that teased his face like feathers, he imagined this woman was a heartbreaker.

Or had she had her heart broken? By him?

Twenty minutes later, they exited into a familiar neighborhood. The trees were a little taller and thicker and the roads had been repaved, but the stately brick mansions and estates that flanked St. Aloysius High School were too arrogant and ostentatious to be forgotten.

She slowed down before she jumped a curb and motored down an unpaved drive that ran parallel to the school's six-foot stone wall. He hadn't been back to the scene of his many crimes since graduation and he certainly never expected to return with an anonymous classmate with unclear intentions.

Though as far as intentions went, the mysterious kind were often the most interesting.

"Glad to be back?"

Now that the engine no longer roared in his ears, he heard a familiar cadence in her voice. Oh, yeah. He knew her. He knew a lot of girls back in high school, both casually and biblically—usually both. And yet, somehow, he didn't think she was one of his many conquests. Something about the confident way she engaged the kickstand and slid off the leather seat told him she was more of a mystery than a blast from his past.

He hopped off and stared down the dirt path. The access drive at St. Aloysius High School, barely wide enough to accommodate the golf cart he'd regularly appropriate from the ground's staff, had been the scene of quite a few memories, both good and bad.

"I couldn't get out of this place fast enough," he confessed.

She laughed. "I remember that about you."

She unhooked her helmet, but didn't remove it.

"Wish I could say what I remember about you."

"Maybe you won't remember me at all," she said, but he could hear the tease in her voice.

That voice.

While he dug deep into his memory to place the familiar sound, she grabbed a low branch and pulled herself up onto the stone wall in three easy moves. She straddled the wall while he wrestled with a suspicion that couldn't possibly be true.

Could it?

Rip grabbed the branch and propelled himself onto the fence beside her. He mimicked her position, scooting forward so that his jeans scraped against the rough texture in a not-unpleasant way. When their knees touched, she pulled off her helmet and let it drop to the loamy ground.

A curtain of dark hair cascaded past her shoulders. She combed her fingers through her slick locks, then faced him, looking at once mussed and perfect.

"I'm the last girl you expected, aren't I?"

He tried to reply, but barely managed a nod. She further sealed his silence by grabbing his cheeks and tugging his face to hers so that their lips were less than an inch apart.

"Then prepare for the unexpected."

Of all the girls he'd gone to school with, of all the women he'd enjoyed since he'd ridden out of town, he'd never in a million years expected to be face-to-face—or lips to lips— with the girl most likely to turn his ass down.

## 2

---

SHE KISSED HIM. SHE didn't think, didn't overanalyze, didn't overorchestrate the touching of lips that she'd been anticipating for over nine months, ever since Scott "Rip" Ripley had checked the Yes box on the invitation to their ten-year class reunion.

The planning was over—and the party had begun.

With her mind, body and soul open, she surrendered to the dizzying sensations that came from finally taking what she had wanted for so very, very long.

Just as she expected, he tasted like sweet cola and freedom and forbidden lust. The warmth of his tongue as it swirled around hers possessed enough heat to melt asphalt.

She gripped tight to the stone wall beneath her. Grit bit into her skin with an exquisite pain that kept her from going too far, too fast. Not that she hadn't already gone further and faster than she ever expected.

"Erica," he murmured, his mouth still pressed to hers.

"Mmm?"

"Holt?"

"Mmm-hmm," she verified.

"What are you doing?" he asked, skimming his lips across

her cheeks, down her chin, and then along the ridge of her jawline.

God, he was good. Oh, so good.

"Kissing you," she replied.

"Yes, you are." He wiped his hands on the thighs of his jeans, then speared them into her hair and repositioned her face so that she had no choice but look at him directly—without lip contact. "But why?"

She blinked. Was it her imagination, or was his jaw more square-shaped now than it had been all those years ago? His eyes looked even bluer. As it had been in the past, his hair was longer than the St. Aloysius dress code requirements allowed—and it still suited him.

"Why?" she repeated. "Because it's long overdue."

She kissed him again and for a second time, he didn't resist. Ten years clearly had changed the man. When she'd tried this last time, he'd pushed her away and forever ended their secret, albeit totally platonic friendship.

The memory shouldn't have been so fresh, but ten minutes or ten years couldn't erase what had become a singular moment in her senior year. She could feel the bite of the torn leather booth against the back of her thighs and could still smell the greasy pepperoni and cigarette smoke in the South Side pizza parlor where they'd met for her French lessons.

In his old neighborhood, no one would recognize them. No one who saw them together would talk or spread rumors or better yet, intrude. No one who'd witnessed her spontaneous attempt to kiss him—which he'd spurned before her lips had touched his—would ever report that St. Aloysius's good girl had attempted to seduce the ultimate bad boy.

And had failed.

But she wasn't failing now. This kiss was everything she'd wanted ten years ago. Tentative, yet passionate. Unexpected, yet natural. Forbidden, yet undeniable.

Until he broke away.

Again.

"You're playing with fire," he warned.

She smiled. "God, I hope so."

She moved in for another kiss, but this time, he caught her by the upper arms.

"Holt, you need to slow down."

She narrowed her eyes. "And you need a new script. That's exactly what you said to me our senior year before you stopped returning my calls."

He scooted away from her, swung his leg over so that he was facing the school grounds and after throwing her a wary glance, launched himself onto the carefully tended lawn.

"I did you a favor," he insisted, punching a finger in her direction.

The gesture pushed her over the edge—literally and figuratively. She jumped off the wall with a little more force than necessary and when one heel caught the ground at an odd angle, she dropped to her knees, blindsided by a burst of pain in her ankle.

He was beside her in an instant, cursing even as he braced her foot.

"Can you move?"

She inhaled and exhaled until the tiny bursts of light in her eyes disappeared. "I'm fine. I just twisted it a little."

"Let me check." He felt around for the zipper that ran up the back of the boot, but as much as she didn't mind having his hands on her, she wasn't done being angry yet.

She yanked out of his grasp and rubbed her joint through the leather. "I said I'm fine. Did anyone ever tell you that you're bossy?"

He scowled at her. "As I recall, you cornered the market on bossy a long time ago."

"And what? You find bossiness unattractive?"

"Right," he snapped, "like anything about you is unattractive."

Erica grunted when her fingers dug into a sore spot. "Well, you were all hot and ready to go on a wild adventure with the sexy, anonymous biker chick. You even climbed a damned tree to find out who I was. The second you saw it was me, you put on the brakes. What am I supposed to think?"

"Not the *second*," he countered, dropping from his knees to his ass, as if her pointing out the truth had thrown him off balance.

Well, maybe it had. She had very little idea about what his life had been like since graduation, but she knew he hadn't joined the priesthood or become a monk. His aunt and uncle still socialized with her family, so she knew he'd served in Afghanistan and had returned unharmed. She knew he'd graduated from college and that he lived in New York City.

Beyond that, his life was a mystery as much as hers likely was to him.

But it had been that mystery that had inspired her to jump completely out of her comfort zone. Around the same time she'd learned Rip was coming to the reunion, Erica had watched her normally cautious, infinitely serious best friend, Abby, lose her mind over a mysterious man from her past. At the time, Erica had thought Abby was making a huge mistake opening her heart to a man with a shady past—but in the end, Abby had found the love of her life.

She'd taken a risk. She'd gone against conventional wisdom and as a result, exchanged loneliness for delirious happiness.

Erica didn't expect the same outcome for herself. She wasn't looking for a soul mate. For tonight, for the weekend, she just wanted to have some fun.

Even though she was one of young Chicago's most sought after event planners, Erica's life was anything but entertaining. She worked twelve-hour days during the week and on the weekend of a wedding, charity gala or anniversary dinner, a sixteen-hour day was a luxury. In her pitiful free time, she'd searched for love in all the right places—in college, at the clubs, during the parties she planned for doctors, attorneys, bankers and corporate CEOs. She'd even been engaged—three times—but she'd never made it down the aisle.

Without a lot of time for a social life that wasn't bought and paid for, Erica had chosen the same kind of guys she dated in high school. The kind she had no trouble taking home to her parents. But though her fiancés had all been great friends, none made her life different or better.

She didn't want the same-old, same-old. She wanted more.

With Rip, she could get that—if only for a weekend. Fresh off a wild, sexy experience, she could break her bad dating habits in a big way. She wasn't looking for an engagement ring or a trip to the altar.

She wanted to shake up the foundation of her life, starting with the sex.

When she'd first made up her mind to pursue Rip, she'd been invigorated and anxious, just as she had when they'd made their secret pact for him to tutor her in French. Now, she felt exactly the same way that she had on the humiliating afternoon when he'd refused to kiss her.

Stupid, unattractive and out of her league.

"I'm sorry," she said, pushing his hand away when he tried to help her stand. She got herself into this ridiculous mess; she was going to have to get herself out. She tested her ankle and as she suspected, the pain had diminished. At least the expensive boots had been worth the cost. She wasn't so sure about the ultimate price to her ego.

"Don't be sorry," he said. "I'm the one who's acting like an idiot. Old habits die hard."

She locked her gaze with his, trying not to let the sheer beauty of his baby blues distract her from gauging his honesty. He wore repentance well. But then, he probably had a lot of practice.

She shifted her weight to one hip and crossed her arms. "Why did you push me away?"

"Then or now?" he asked.

"We'll start with then and if I like your answer, we'll move on to now."

"See?" he said, gesturing toward her, the corner of his mouth quirking into a surprisingly boyish grin. "Bossy."

She arched a brow and he acquiesced, but not without a self-deprecating chuckle.

"Why did I resist kissing the irresistible Erica Holt? You were too good for me."

She clucked her tongue. "That's bullshit."

"No, it wasn't," he insisted, his voice deep with conviction. "Not then. Hell, probably not now, either. This may come as a huge shock to you, but I was a player back in high school."

She faked surprise with an overly dramatic gasp. "No! Tell me it isn't true!"

"Smart-ass," he grumbled.

She poked him in the chest, taking advantage of the opportunity to touch him, even if only with the tip of her finger. "You never would have said that to me ten years ago."

"Yes, I would have," he argued. "As I recall, I called you worse on several occasions while we were inhaling the double meat pies at Aurelio's Pizza. You were a closeted smart-ass who put on her best game face at school and had all the teachers and administrators fooled into thinking you were a perfect little princess."

She resisted the urge to gag and instead, took a tentative step closer to him. The ache in her ankle was gone, zapped out of her system by the direction of their conversation.

"Are you admitting that there might have been more to me than met the eye? That during our French lessons, you realized that I wasn't just a one-dimensional, candy-coated good girl who couldn't be sullied by the likes of, I don't know, *you?*"

She watched his jaw twitch and his cheeks hollow out as he sucked in a breath of frustration. When he shook his head but didn't reply, she smiled.

Button pushed.

"Don't put words in my mouth," he chastised.

"That wasn't what I wanted to put in your mouth, but you haven't left me any other choice."

The shock on his face gave her the jolt she needed to spread her fingers over his T-shirt, marveling in the feel of the rockhard pecs underneath. The muscled tightness continued up to his shoulders, where her dark fingernails scraped against the skin of his neck and jaw.

She watched his Adam's apple undulate in his throat as he swallowed hard. "You really want to do this?"

God, he had a sexy voice, especially when it possessed that strangled sound a man made when he knew he should resist, but couldn't.

"Don't I deserve a little fun?" She skimmed her thumbs over the curves of his ears. "I'm not an innocent Catholic schoolgirl anymore, Rip. Or haven't you noticed?"

His gazed dipped down to where her leather vest gapped, revealing more than a generous view of her breasts.

He licked his lips. "I noticed."

Boldly, she curved her neck back and slowly pulled down the zipper to reveal her bra. Her move broke the last of his control. With a strangled growl, he pulled her close and suckled her throat, one hand braced on the small of her back while the other tangled into her hair. The sensation of his tongue and teeth striking down the tendons of her neck ignited a madness Erica had only dreamed of. He was so assured. So precise. Just the right amount of pressure. Just the right degree of moisture. Just the right level of hungered sound to let her know that her transformation from pampered princess to sexy seductress had been worth the effort.

Or would be. Soon. Very, very soon.

She tugged the strands of his hair, guiding him lower, to the edges of her collarbone, to the valley between her breasts. His tongue darted into the shadowed triangle, tracing just above the curve of satin.

Suddenly, the leather vest felt hot and confining. As if he'd read her mind, he lowered the zipper all the way and buried his face between the dark flaps.

"Oh, yes," she murmured when he blew a hot breath over her.

"I knew you'd be perfect," he said. "I always knew."

She shook her head, but kept her denial to herself. She wasn't perfect—she was the opposite of perfect. She was flawed and needful and in most of the places he touched with his lips, empty. But the pressure of his body against hers and the raucousness of his need filled her with passion. With fire.

With demands she expected him to meet, sooner rather than later.

# 3

For every cell in his body that ignited with pure, sexual need, another one zapped warning signals to his brain that told him to stop this madness. Erica Holt was innocent. Unattainable. Better left unsullied by the likes of him, especially when he had no intention of sticking around Chicago once the headmaster declared the Class of 2002 to be graduates of St. Aloysius High School.

The alarms echoed away quickly, part of a decade-old system he'd built to make sure he didn't mess around with a girl who deserved so much better. But this wasn't their senior year anymore. He wasn't the bad boy about to ride out of town on his Harley and leave Chicago behind for good.

Or was he? He'd returned for the reunion, but come Monday, he'd be on his way back to New York, to the work and responsibilities that had transformed his shady past into memories that drove him—memories he could face in the mornings when he looked in the mirror and saw his father's jawline and his mother's eyes.

And man, Erica sure had changed. Judging by the way she tangled her tongue with his, thrust her hands into his hair and pressed her body close so that the buckle on her belt knocked just below his, she was no longer the pristine paragon of purity he'd made her out to be back in high school. She was sensual, sexy and daring. And she wanted to have some fun. *Needed* to have some fun, judging by all she'd confessed. Who better to provide that than him?

"Let's go inside," she said, panting.

"Inside the school?"

Shock hitched his voice up at the end and the squeak made her laugh. Recovered from her ankle twist, she led him down the raked path toward the school's back entrance.

The fact that she felt comfortable enough to stroll across the sprawling lawns of the campus in little but an open vest, black bra, painted-on jeans and boots was enough to ensure his compliance. When they reached the back portico, she released his hand.

"So," she asked, her gray eyes twinkling with mischief. "How are we going to get in?"

"Don't you have a key? Aren't you like a trustee or something?"

"Oh, come on," she cajoled. "What's the fun in going in the proper way? Besides—" she held her hands out wide "—I don't exactly have excessive room for keys and pass codes."

"It's alarmed now?"

Her smile told him she meant for this to be a challenge.

He could only imagine his uncle's lined face if he got a call now, ten years after graduation, explaining how his nephew once again needed to be bailed out of trouble. Judging by her lack of fear, though, he suspected she was more than up to the task of talking them out of an arrest should they get caught.

He grabbed her hand. "This way."

Rip jogged down the stairs and scanned the brick wall, both surprised and pleased that the school hadn't changed the light fixtures since graduation. They were still old and rusted, still hinged in a way that made them excellent for hiding things. He counted two over from the center, then unscrewed the base and retrieved the spiny skeleton key.

"Why am I not surprised that you know where Mr. Foster hid that?" she asked.

"This school didn't have many secrets from me," he replied.

"Least of all secret passageways where you could lure your willing, female classmates."

He tugged her behind the row of thick yew bushes that blocked the entrance to the storage space tucked beneath the porch. "This place was too grimy for chicks, though I did duck in here to read my most subversive materials."

The key worked. He opened the door and waited for a beep, screech or wail that would mean they'd been busted, but Erica boldly brushed by him.

"It's not wired," she said. "I had to come down here last week to retrieve our old class banner for the party tonight. I just wanted to see if you'd lost your nerve."

He jogged back outside to replace the key, then came back in and locked the door. "You're full of surprises, Erica Holt."

From underneath the single bulb light fixture, she gave him a saucy wink. "So are you. But you're right. This place *is* too grimy for a rendezvous. And here I had all these fantasies about where you'd go when you didn't show up for class."

He tried not to let her confession boost his ego. He had been popular with his female classmates, but only because he put a little more effort than his male counterparts into making sure he wasn't the only one getting a thrill out of a make-out session.

He leaned his shoulder against a rusted metal shelving unit and shoved it aside. A bucket filled with musty rags toppled off and the stacks of boxes jostled a layer of dust into the air that made them both cough.

Behind the shelf, a sliver of a window shined down just

enough natural light onto an old broken desktop. Man, he'd spent hours down here, hiding from the dean of students and soaking up his real education from sources as diverse as *Popular Mechanics* and *Food & Wine* magazine.

"Sorry to disappoint you, but this wasn't my romantic rendezvous spot. This was my private haven. The headmaster never could figure out where I'd disappear to when I was supposed to be in chemistry."

"Or how you snuck into the building after hours to change the combinations on the freshmen lockers?"

He turned, ready to insist that he'd never copped to that prank, not even to her, when he watched her disappear behind a stack of crates lined up against the interior wall. Apparently, he wasn't the only one who was privy to the school's "alternate" entrances. By the time he put the storeroom back in order, she'd pried open the rusty door that led first into the maintenance closet and then into the school.

His eyes quickly adjusted to the darkness and his ears reverberated with the sound of her sexy boots marching without hesitation down the empty hall. The Erica Holt he'd resisted back in high school would never have bent a blade of grass on school grounds without written permission from the headmaster and board of governors. That she was now breaking and entering without a hint of fear fired his imagination to dangerous levels.

He'd never thought he'd see her like this. He never thought he'd want to. When she'd tried to kiss him at the pizza parlor their senior year, he'd called on every ounce of his self-control to resist her. He was a player, but a girl like Erica Holt wasn't a plaything. She was the kind of girl you brought home to meet your parents—if you had them. He hadn't wanted to sully her reputation with gossip and whispers and ultimately, heartbreak.

Instead, he limited himself to girls who didn't care what

other people thought about them and who wouldn't be surprised when he moved on.

If there was one thing everyone knew about Rip, it was that he wasn't the stick-around type.

Even though he'd changed his life drastically over the past decade, that part of him hadn't. His relationships never lasted more than a month or two. He steered clear of women who had their sights set on something more.

But Erica wasn't one of those women—not anymore. She wanted a fling. A well-deserved weekend of fun. Over the past ten years, he'd learned how to resist a lot of temptations—but a good girl gone bad?

He was putty in her hands.

He followed her scent into the gleaming halls of St. Aloysius High School.

The place hadn't changed. Same polished marble floors. Same soaring high ceilings. Same metal lockers built stylishly into the walls, painted a matte, muted navy, the only sparkle the polished brass numbers and the occasional plate acknowledging an alumni donation. The hairs on the back of his neck spiked. It took a mental shake and a prolonged look at Erica's sweetly swinging backside to rid himself of the instinct to get the hell out of here while he still could.

"Do you even know where you're going?" he shouted.

Her laughter echoed though the vacant hallway. "I figured we'd hit all the hot spots."

"In this joint? We're not exactly rolling down Rush Street."

"The party isn't in the location, it's in the people. Besides, I don't think you ever truly appreciated the opportunities St. Aloysius had to offer," she said once he'd matched her stride.

"You have heard of Stockholm syndrome, right? I know someone you can talk to about that."

She snorted with a surprising amount of class.

"As if I haven't already spent thousands on therapy."

Rip rubbed his hand over his face, trying to hide the expression of shock that had lifted his eyebrows and dropped his jaw. Seeing Erica dressed like a biker chick was one thing—hearing the bitter undertone was something else.

She caught his shocked expression in her sideways glance.

"Oh, come on. You can't be surprised that a pampered princess like me has been to a psychologist or two."

"I guess I'd be more surprised if you hadn't."

"Because I have so much to be depressed about? Poor little rich girl."

Rip stopped walking. Half of her tone was self-deprecating, but the other half slid under his skin like a splinter. He prided himself on being a nonjudgmental guy and suddenly, this little excursion with the class Goody Two-shoes turned vixen suddenly didn't feel so much like a spontaneous lark.

"Maybe this isn't just about having some fun," he said.

She laughed, grabbed his hand and tugged him forward. "Aw, don't worry, Rip. I'm not getting all serious on you. Once we get back to Celebrations, the reunion is going to be nothing but fun and games for you, but for me, it's going to be all work and no play. Don't I deserve a little wild time now?"

She sped up, practically skipping as she dashed forward, her hand skimming along an uninterrupted expanse of brick between what used to be the library and the classroom designated for detentions—a room he knew entirely too well.

At his burst of energy, she laughed. The sound flooded the empty hallways, prompting him to catch up to her and cup his hand over her mouth.

She licked the inside of his palm. He released her.

"You need to quiet down or we're going to get caught."

She arched a brow.

He laughed. "I can't believe I just said that."

She frowned prettily. "Don't tell me you've gone all upstanding and law-abiding now. That wouldn't be any fun at all."

She jumped forward, kissed him on the chin, then dashed farther down the hall. When she reached the south staircase, she grabbed the worn, round finial and swung her hips in a provocative pose that dispersed the tension in his shoulders and pushed it farther down so that the crotch of his jeans suddenly felt very confining.

"Here I am running around a large, deserted space in nothing but a bra and the baddest bad boy in the senior class doesn't even try to cop a feel."

Her saucy retort caught him up short. "Maybe I'm not the baddest bad boy anymore."

She twisted her body so that her sweet ass swung in his direction. "Maybe not, but I'm not interested in being the best little good girl, so come over here and show me exactly what you used to do underneath these stairs."

So she did know his hot spots. Before he changed his mind, he tugged her into the shadowy spot beneath the stairs where he'd spent a lot of his time between classes—only here, he was rarely alone.

Like the hideout they'd used to sneak into the school, the area was cramped and shadowed, a slanted space with plenty of room for storage and some good, old-fashioned messing around.

Erica flattened herself into the farthest corner and leaned provocatively against her hands. With her arms tucked behind her, her barely contained breasts arched against the cups of her dark, satin bra.

"Did you have sex underneath here?"

"What do you think?"

"No," she answered matter-of-factly, her gaze assessing him while she chewed on the corner of her bottom lip. "I always suspected some seriously heavy petting, though."

"You had a very naughty mind."

Her gaze flared. "A naughty mind was all I could have. Though you know," she said, locking her hands onto the underside of the step above her. "There's an echo. Screams of ecstasy should have been heard all the way down the hall if you were doing it right."

"Maybe I wasn't doing it right," he teased.

"If you hadn't been, girls wouldn't have spent so much time trying to get you to take them to second base and beyond back here."

He clucked his tongue in mock disapproval. "I never figured you for the type who listened to gossip."

"You never figured me for a lot of things," she corrected.

"My mistake." He shrugged out of his jacket and joined her against the wall where the rising stairs gave him just enough head room to trap her in the tight space. "I don't have a lot of regrets about high school. Can't afford them. But turning you down? I'm suddenly realizing that was a huge error on my part."

His confession brightened her eyes so that the thunderous gray took on an irresistible silver gleam. "Now you can make it right," she taunted. "I promise to be quiet."

Rip slid his hand into the tight space between them and hooked his finger beneath the strap of her bra. He hadn't come back to Chicago to undo his past mistakes, but now that he was here with a warm and willing woman, he had no means to resist.

"I don't think so. Now that I've got you under this stairwell, I want you to make as much noise as possible."

# 4

She thought she would lose her mind.

Rip's lazy trail up from her waist to the underside of her breasts turned his touch into concentrated torture. Finger by finger, inch by inch, he blazed a path over her nerve endings until each fired the neurons in her brain to cry for more, more, more. When he unhooked her bra and touched the lower crescent of her areola, she hissed at the burst of pleasure.

"See," he said, circling the dark oval with the calloused tip of his thumb. "That's the kind of sound, back in high school, I would have muffled with a kiss."

"Then kiss me," she said, groaning when he added his forefinger to the mix and plucked her nipple tight.

"Oh, no. We're not kids anymore and no one's around to catch us. You make all the noise you want."

With a loud and hungry growl, he grabbed her ass and lifted her so that he could take her freed nipple into his mouth.

Erica did as she was told, growling out a whimper of pleasure that shattered the silence. She hadn't expected him to go so far so fast—or that she'd melt into him with such complete surrender. She pressed her body hard against the wall and locked her hands behind his neck, grateful he had the power to hold her while the bursts of pleasure stole the strength from her limbs.

"This...isn't...second...base," she protested, her breath shallow as pure bliss ping-ponged from nerve pleasure point to pleasure point.

"It is in the big leagues," he murmured before switching sides and invoking the same incredible sensations on her other breast.

Erica laughed, losing herself in the sensations. Yes, this little corner of St. Aloysius was practically the Wrigley Field of sexual encounters—and Rip was an all-star. And though she'd never done anything so bold or brazen, she wasn't exactly a little leaguer. He might have caught her off guard, but she was in this to win it.

She grasped his T-shirt, bunching the material in her hands as he increased the pleasurable pain he inflicted on her breasts. When he broke away to kiss a path up her neck, she ripped his shirt off and tossed it to the floor. He unwound the satiny straps of her bra off her body, and then lifted her higher so she could wrap her legs around his waist. Together, they fell back against the wall, their mouths fused while their hands groped and grabbed, pleasured and explored.

"God, you're hot," he groaned, his breath steamy against the tendons of her neck.

"Pot, meet kettle," she replied.

His muscles were rock-hard, his skin smooth except for the hair on his chest that she followed like a trail with her touch, tracing the downward line to where it disappeared in the waistband of his jeans. She unclipped his belt and popped the button, and impatiently ran her hand down his erection through the denim, her body thrumming as her brain made the intimate calculations about his size and level of hardness.

Her sex throbbed and ached. He was perfect. Or he would be, once she got his jeans off.

The sound of his zipper rasped in harmony with the huff and puff of heavy breathing and smack and suckle of hungry, wet kisses. When she wrapped her hand around his sex, his groan merged with her squeal of pleasure.

"Erica," he begged.

His skin was silky, hot and rock-solid. She ran her hand up and down, loving how each stroke turned his erection to steel even as it loosened the muscles in his shoulders. He set her down and braced his hands on the wall on either side of her to keep himself upright while she gave him her full attention.

"Mmm," she said, humming her appreciation against his neck. "Now I have you right where I want you."

"At this point, sweetheart, you can have me wherever you want me."

Trouble was, she wanted him everywhere. She wanted his hands on her body, his mouth on her nipples and his erection between her legs, sliding into her hot, wet flesh. But this space was too confined, too cramped. Luckily, they had the whole school at their disposal and despite her claims otherwise, she did indeed know of several ways to get into places where they could finish what they'd started.

Maybe the teacher's lounge?

The library?

"Who's in here?"

The voice boomed across the empty halls, freezing them both in place.

Shocked, Erica tightened her grip until he grunted. Finger by finger, she released him, trying not to rustle the fabric of his jeans or even breathe too loudly.

"I know I heard something," the voice muttered.

The jangle of keys covered the sound of Rip securing his pants. When they heard a classroom door creak open, followed by the clicking of lights and the retreat of footsteps, they hurriedly dressed, though Erica put on her vest without her bra, which she couldn't find. Rip grabbed her hand and guided her down into the lowest, darkest corner underneath the stairs.

"Security guard," he whispered.

Erica squeezed her eyes shut tight. Mr. Abernathy had been working the grounds of St. Aloysius for nearly fifty years, a fact she knew because she was on the alumni committee planning to honor him at the beginning of the next school year. If he caught her here, she'd never be able to look him in the eye, much less present him with an engraved watch in front of the entire student body.

"Oh, God," she whimpered.

Rip, however, was grinning from ear to ear.

Again, the keys jangled. Again, the boots shuffled over the marble. This time, they heard the punching in of an electronic code. He was either going into the library or the front office, the only two rooms on this floor that were wired for security.

Rip grabbed his jacket. "This is our chance, bad girl. Ready to make a break for it?"

"What?"

He didn't give her time to think or plan or strategize. He yanked her out of their hiding place then led her as quietly and quickly as possible up to the second floor.

"We'll never get out this way," she admonished once she was certain they were out of earshot. At least the second floor had carpeting in the halls, muffling the sound of their shoes.

He stopped long enough to flash a cocky grin. "Are you seriously doubting my knowledge of this building?"

"You haven't been here for ten years!" she reminded him, her exasperation crisp even if her voice was hushed.

"Nothing changes in this place. Come on."

To her shock and consternation, he was right. He dragged her to the fire exit and disengaged the alarm with four flicks from his pocketknife. They hurried down the stairs and

waited in the musty darkness for Mr. Abernathy to exit the
main office before they made a beeline for the library. Once
he was inside, they dashed across the hall and left the way
they'd come in, though they huddled behind the yew bushes
to catch their breaths and make sure they weren't spotted before dashing across the lawn.

"I can't believe we almost got caught," she said.

Rip chuckled. "There's a lot about this afternoon that I
can't believe, and the fact that we weren't spotted doesn't
even rank in the top ten."

Ten minutes later, Mr. Abernathy zoomed past them on his
golf cart. When they were certain he'd turned the corner to
do a full perimeter sweep, they ran full-out for the wall. Rip
cupped his hands together to give her a boost, then launched
himself up and over with skill that testified to his physical
prowess and vast experience.

Once on the other side, Erica flattened herself against the
wall, her lungs burning. Sweat glued her vest to her bare
breasts and flushed her skin with heat nearly equal to what
she'd experienced underneath the stairs with Rip.

Nearly, but not quite.

Before she had the power to move, he was kissing her
again. He tasted of salt and excitement and not an ounce of
regret. She clutched his shoulders, needing one last injec-
tion of his special kind of carelessness to get her through the
next test of the weekend—showing up at the resort with Rip.

He slid his hands over her hips. "When you plan a party,
woman, you plan a party."

From down the drive, she heard a strange hum heading
toward them.

Golf cart?

Rip grabbed her helmet and handed it to her while he
jumped on the bike.

"Too bad the party's over," she said, climbing on behind him and wrapping her hands tight around his middle.

"Party's only beginning," he yelled over the engine.

With expert precision, Rip pushed her Harley to the limit. Gravel and dirt kicked up around them and despite the shouts from Mr. Abernathy, who'd just rounded the corner, he tore down the drive with more speed than she ever would have risked, took them airborne over the curb and then popped a wheelie as he sped toward the highway.

Erica squealed, held on tight and let him drive.

WHEN THE RESORT CAME into view, Rip felt Erica lean her cheek into the space between his shoulder blades. Waves of her emotion seeped through his T-shirt and jacket—emotions that countered the whoops and squeals she'd made when he rode her bike the way it was meant to be ridden.

Now, her arms, squeezed tight around his middle, gave off a pensive vibe that was entirely counter to goal for the weekend. She'd said she wanted no strings, wild and crazy fun. But he supposed the closer she got to her old classmates and professional responsibilities, the harder it was for her to hang on to saucy, carefree intentions.

Dusk had begun darkening the clear summer sky so that the fancy gold lights on the canopied entrance sparkled like rhinestones. He eased the bike to a stop a good forty yards from where bellmen hustled to unload the luggage from the half dozen cars and taxis lining the drive, powered down and shifted his weight to keep the bike upright while he waited for her to pull away.

She didn't move.

He relaxed, not realizing until that moment how much he'd tensed.

"I wish I didn't have to go," he heard her mutter.

He slid his palm over her hands, which were still gripping

his belt buckle. She was shaking. He twisted around, his fingers tight over hers.

"Party can't start without you," he pointed out.

She sighed. "That's me. The mastermind of big events. Give me a party to plan and an unlimited budget and I can make all your dreams come true."

"Most of my dreams have nothing to do with big parties," he teased.

It took a moment of maneuvering, but he finally found the right angle that allowed him to kiss her without removing her helmet. In seconds, he was drunk off the flavor of her mouth, the texture of her tongue and the sweet pressure of her lips.

"Mine, either," she said. "But once I go through those revolving doors, the fantasy ends."

"It doesn't have to."

She glanced at the hotel entrance, her stare a mixture of resignation and reluctance. "Doesn't it? It's one thing being myself around you, but once I see all those old faces, I'll be that same old girl Erica I used to be. Efficient and prissy. Always organizing the fun instead of having any."

He turned around to face her before powering the bike up again. She wore her regrets like some women wore big, gaudy jewelry.

"You don't have to be that girl anymore."

She sighed, reaching up to touch his cheek with a quivering hand. "It was easy to break the cycle with you. I'm not sure how to do it with everyone else."

Rip closed his eyes and in a split second, his instincts kicked an idea into his brain that might just do the trick. When he looked at her again, she must have recognized that he was up to something because she was grinning ear to ear.

"Do you trust me?" he asked.

She snuggled in close behind him, her body quivering with what he hoped was anticipation.

"Yes," she confirmed.

He revved the Harley. "Then leave this to me. By the time this weekend is over, your reputation is going to be good and sullied."

She squeezed him tighter and made that little high-pitched squeal that he couldn't wait to hear once he finally had her in bed.

# 5

"WAIT, IS TONIGHT a masquerade?"

Kate Schaffer, Erica's assistant, frantically brushed at the screen of her digital tablet, the bright red frames of her glasses sliding halfway down her nose. "I don't have anything in my notes about a costume party. If you texted me about the change, I didn't receive it. Unless, wait, I believe there is a costume rental facility on property. I think I might have passed it when I was doing our first walk-through. I'll go and—"

Erica threw an apologetic look at Rip, then grabbed her assistant by the arm and led her to a corner of the hotel lobby. Apparently, Kate had missed their grand entrance—one that had resulted in a burst of applause from Rip's old gang, followed by an audible gasp when she'd ripped off her helmet and he'd kissed her in front of God and everyone.

It had been glorious.

The taste of his tongue tangling with hers had been sweeter than all the others they'd shared this afternoon, combined. She supposed it was selfish and shallow for her to revel in the shock on her former classmates' faces, but she couldn't help it. To make an omelet, you had to break some eggs—and she and Rip had just scrambled enough for a banquet.

"I'm not dressed like this for a costume party," she said, catching sight of Rip's back as he made his way to the registration desk. She already had a suite for the weekend, so she'd suggested he cancel his reservation. He'd seemed to like the idea, but hadn't said if he was going to do it before Kate had come tearing through the guests in a panic. "Tonight's mixer is casual, just like we planned. I just went out for a…a joyride."

Kate pushed her glasses up and squared her shoulders. Dressed in one of her vintage 1940s pin-striped suits with a sweetheart neckline and a pencil skirt that emphasized her curves, she looked half like the intimidating lawyer she used to be and half like a femme fatale from a Sam Spade film. If anyone was dressed for a Halloween-themed party, it was Kate. She just had the nerve to do it every day.

Hiring a former partner at Weinstein, Hobbes and Madison as her second-in-command at Events by Erica had been a risk. Kate was used to being in charge and Erica had doubts that she'd take kindly to someone younger than her giving her direction. But when she'd enticed one of the city's best chefs to cater a dinner for forty-two on two days' notice and claimed she'd work for one-tenth her former salary, Erica had taken the gamble. Since that move over a year ago, Kate had become an invaluable employee and a good friend—one who would, ultimately, understand Erica's need to make drastic changes to her increasingly unsatisfactory life.

"You went out on that death trap on two wheels again?" Kate asked.

Erica lifted her chin. "And if I did?"

"As long as you signed that insurance policy I took out on you, you can do whatever the hell you want."

Erica shook her head. "I'm a very safe rider and before you start mimicking my mother and saying it's not me you worry about, but everyone else on the road—"

"God help me if I ever start sounding like your mother...
or anyone's mother. It's your life, but should you risk it when
we don't have a full weekend of events to coordinate?"

"Yeah, about that," Erica said, glancing across the lobby
in search of her new hero, who was suddenly nowhere to be
seen. "How much do I *actually* have to be involved in the mi-
nutiae of the reunion at this point?"

Kate's pencil-enhanced brows arched high over her wide
amber eyes. "You wiped out on your bike, didn't you?" She
grabbed Erica's helmet and inspected it for dents, scratches
or cracks.

"No," Erica said, yanking the helmet away and hating how
her voice pitched guiltily. She never, ever left Kate in charge
of an entire event, not because her assistant wasn't entirely
capable, but because Erica loved her job and had never wanted
to be anywhere except in the middle of the action.

Now, however, the only action she wanted to be in the
middle of was in her bed with Rip.

Sharing the ride up to the school, sneaking into the building, making out under the stairs and nearly getting caught
by Mr. Abernathy had been a powerful aphrodisiac. For the
first time in recent memory, Erica had felt like she could take
on the world—not because she was organized and prepared
and efficient, but because she'd let go of long-held fears and
surrendered instead to her dreams and desires. The residual
buzz of that power still zinged through her veins, enhanced
by Rip's outrageous entrance. She only wished more of her
old classmates had been around to see it.

Well, they'd get an eyeful later at the opening night party.

If they made it to the party.

A wolf whistle from behind skittered up Erica's spine. She
wasn't used to attracting this kind of attention, but then, she
wasn't dressed in skintight jeans and a low-cut leather vest
every day, either.

Luckily, the whistler was a friend, a man who'd always known there was more to her than her good girl image, but who'd never held it against her.

"Now, that's more like it," Shaw Tyler growled, his after-sex voice as smooth and confident as when he was singing on stage. He walked lazily across to where she and Kate stood in the corner, placed his hand on the small of her back and nearly let his fingers drop onto her ass as he kissed her on the cheek.

"Here's the Erica Holt I always wanted to see."

He gave her a long, appreciative once-over. She might have slugged him except they'd been friends since they were kids. He'd always encouraged her to dress a little more provocatively and act a little less like a benevolent dictator, but Erica had pushed his suggestions aside. The son of a record executive and a famous chanteuse, Shaw's life had never had the same expectations as hers. He couldn't understand how hard it was to break out of the box when he'd never owned a box to begin with.

"Well, take a good look then," Erica replied, pecking his cheek in return. "I'm on my way upstairs to change."

"Need help?"

Kate groaned, but Erica didn't flinch. Shaw was a shameless flirt. She guessed that the reason they'd remained friends was because she'd always been immune to his charms. The Tyler family loved to buy properties and the Holt family loved to sell them. As a result, she and Shaw had known each other long enough for this game to be old, worn-out and devoid of any real sexual tension.

"I've got it, thanks," she assured him.

"You sure? Okay, but maybe your hot little assistant here can give you some fashion advice for tonight. She seems to know how to dress to…impress."

Erica stepped between them. Shaw, like her, was eight years younger than her assistant, but that never seemed to stop his over-the-top come-ons. Unfortunately, they didn't go over as well with the former attorney as they did with Erica. In fact, every time Erica hired Shaw's band, Cell Block Tango, to play at an event, Kate made a thousand excuses to ensure that she had little, if anything, to do with interacting with the lead singer.

"Turn it down a notch, Shaw," she warned. "I'm handing over the reins of the whole reunion to my gorgeous assistant and I don't need her wound up and distracted."

"He doesn't distract me," Kate protested.

Shaw licked his lips. "But I do wind you up. Admit that much, babe."

Kate lifted her tablet chest-high, as if tempted to bash Shaw over the head with it. Erica pushed Shaw out of the way. "Don't you have to set up for the sound check or something?"

"Aw, come on, Katie-gate," he said, unrepentant. "You know I'm only trying to get under your skin."

Erica watched her assistant's nearly imperceptible blush brighten to scarlet. Shaw had started using the ridiculous nickname with her assistant the first time they'd met and even though it riled her up—or maybe *because* it riled her up—he continued to use it even though she'd asked him a thousand times not to.

"Mr. Tyler," she replied coolly. "I suggest you get to work if you wish to receive your payment on time. If Erica's truly putting me in charge, then she won't object to my invoking the noncompliance clause in your contract that gives me the right to deduct from our agreed-upon fee if your performance isn't up to *my* expectations."

Erica wasn't surprised by how powerful Kate sounded when she turned up her attorney knob, but she couldn't help widening her eyes and staring at Shaw in warning.

He, of course, merely winked then turned with all serious-ness to Kate, his arms crossed and chin tilted at a contemplative angle. "I get the impression you don't like me, Katie-gate. It wounds me to the core."

"I sincerely doubt you have a core," she snapped.

Shaw opened his mouth to lob another of his undoubtedly clever retorts, but Erica cut him off. Shaw and Kate had clashed each and every time she hired him to play one of her events. Normally, she found it entertaining, but as the lobby was starting to fill up with her former classmates and she wanted to find Rip and get upstairs before they were further waylaid, she took Shaw by the arm and led him toward the service elevators, where his band was loading their equipment.

"Your guys know where to set up, right?" she asked. "The rooftop club is very intimate and the acoustics are amazing for an open-air venue. I'll have Kate grab the hotel's sound technician and they'll meet you for a run-through, okay?"

Shaw shot Kate a predatory look, then did as Erica suggested, leaving her assistant with smoke practically pluming out of her diamond-studded ears. Erica should have told him to back off. She needed Kate on her A game. No distractions. No unnecessary conflict. But she wasn't in the mood to put a damper on anyone's sexual mood, least of all her own.

The minute the elevator doors closed on Shaw and his bandmates, Kate charged over.

"I'm sorry, Kate," she said. "I know that Shaw gets a kick out of pushing all your buttons, but I really need—"

Kate waved away her apology. "Who is that?"

"Who?" she asked, turning back to the elevator. "The new guy in Shaw's band? I think his name is Richie. He's a bass guitarist or something."

"Not him," Kate said with a frown. "Him."

She tilted her head to the other side of the lobby, inconspicuously gesturing toward a crowd of men in the lobby. A group of old friends were hugging and laughing and making introductions of wives and girlfriends.

And Rip was standing in the center of the melee, paying attention to none of it.

He was staring straight at her—straight through her, even. The intensity of his gaze reignited the flame he'd sparked under the stairwell and liquefied the desire she'd hoped to keep under control, at least while they were in public.

"He looks like he'd like to eat you for dinner," Kate remarked. "Ex-boyfriend?"

"No," Erica said, an electric thrill shooting its way through her system. "Just an old friend."

"He looks like he'd like to change that," Kate commented.

Erica's mouth watered. "Yeah," she agreed. "He does. And I'm not about to object."

ONLY WHEN RIP'S KNUCKLES started to ache did he realize he was clenching his fists. A raging, fiery emotion coursed through his system—a feeling so unfamiliar, it took him a full minute to recognize it for what it was.

Jealousy.

Green-eyed, dangerous and undeniable.

Shaw Tyler—he'd recognized him easily since the dude hadn't changed one iota since high school—had put his hands on Erica. He'd kissed her. It had only been a brief smack on the cheek. Nothing to get possessive over.

But it wasn't the kiss that had sparked his ire. It was the comfortable familiarity between them. The way her shoulders relaxed and her smile came easily and without any agenda. With him, she was and probably always had been exactly who she'd always been. Not Erica the good girl or Erica the student body president, just Erica, the woman who was sexy, confident and strong.

He'd always known this about her, even if he'd never let

on. He'd made the discovery while watching her from a distance in high school, studying her when she wasn't aware, when she'd drop her guard just enough for a careful observer to recognize telltale expressions, looks and movements of a girl who had more depth than she showed, more desires than she expressed.

Maybe that was why he hadn't been able to resist the chance to tutor her in French. He was pretty sure it explained why he'd continued to meet her at the pizza parlor long after she'd raised her grade. But it definitely was the reason he'd broken things off after her attempt to take their relationship to the next level.

Erica had deserved someone who would cherish her, someone who would bring out the best and sometimes the worst in her and love her all the same. He hadn't been that guy back then.

But he was that guy now.

"Hey, hold that elevator!"

He pushed out of the crowd and jogged across the lobby just as Erica stepped inside, ticking off last-minute instructions to a woman he assumed worked for her. The woman, a striking redhead dressed in an outfit that reminded him of black-and-white movies starring Humphrey Bogart, jumped out of his way with a start.

"Going up?" she asked.

He used every ounce of self-control not to grab her by the hips and pull her hard against him to show her just how *up* he was going.

"Most definitely."

They managed to keep their hands to themselves until after the elevator door closed. Once they were locked away for the fifteen-floor climb to her floor, however, all bets were off. Rip kissed her hard, wrapping his arms tightly around her in a burst of possessiveness that was entirely new to him—and completely addictive.

"Where'd you disappear to?" she asked as he drew a line from her earlobe to the hollow of her neck with his tongue.

"Had to…park…the bike."

She cut into his explanation with moans and coos that spawned his need to get her into her room faster than any elevator could take them. He spared a glance at the numbers. They were nearly there.

Laughing at their own impatience, they jogged down the hall hand in hand. He grabbed the key card from her back pocket, but had to swipe it in the reader twice to get it to work. He pushed his way inside and before the door had swung closed, had her braced against the wall, his mouth on hers. Somewhere in the back of his mind, he heard the clatter of her helmet hitting the carpeted floor, the last sound he recognized before the rush of blood and the pounding of his heartbeat flooded his ears.

"Is this how you want our first time?" he asked, tearing off his jacket and then divesting her of her vest. "Hot? Hard? In the hall?"

"Yes, please," she said, ripping his shirt over his head.

"Thank God."

If not for the task of unlacing their riding boots, they would have been naked in seconds. For a split second, Rip thought about carrying Erica to the bed, but the idea flew out of his mind the minute she spun him up against the wall and dropped to her knees. His mind exploded as she cupped him, stroked him and then took him into her mouth.

The sensations tore him in two. His physical half surrendered to the burst of sensations. Her mouth. Her tongue. Her teeth. The slick, sliding pressure. The tight, humming heat. He tangled his hands into her hair and pressed his full weight against the wall.

The mental half—blinded and confused by the riot of pure pleasure—tried to balk. This was Erica. His Erica. Sweet Erica. Good Erica. Oh-so-good.

"Yes," he muttered, along with an unintelligible string of words that might have made sense in another time and place, but now only sought to spur her deeper, tighter, harder.

When she pulled away with a gasp, he lifted her and swung her around so that they thudded against the wall. She wrapped her legs around his waist, her hot sex wet against his.

"I wasn't…done," she said.

He positioned his thighs and knees, needing just the right leverage to do this right. "Any more done and I wouldn't be able to do this."

He slid inside her. He gave a brief thought to the condom he kept in his wallet and stilled.

"Protection?" he asked.

"Pill," she replied, shifting her hips so that he slid deeper inside her.

"I'm clean," he assured.

"Then do me, Rip. Do me now. Please."

With this plea, all conversation stopped—at least the conversation that existed outside of the language needed to heighten pure, intense pleasure to orgasmic peaks. Everything they said, everything they did, existed in a haze of lust and need and fire. She was tight and hot and loud. He was hard and concentrated and selfish. He wanted her to come and he wanted it now.

Now.

Now.

When she cried out in utter release, he drove harder and faster until his climax exploded through the last of his fantasies. Erica was no longer the good girl he shouldn't touch—she was now the complicated woman he couldn't wait to have again and again and again.

# 6

ERICA SCANNED THE GROWING crowd in the rooftop bar, her skin tingling and her knees a little weak. It had taken what was left of her strength—and there wasn't much to spare—to force her out of the suite in time to give the party space a walk-through and make sure her assistant had not missed a single detail. Which, of course, she hadn't.

But she'd needed the activity of checking to keep her escalating sexual energy from driving her mad. Her afternoon with Rip should have left her satisfied, exhausted and spent. Instead, her nerve endings prickled with renewed awareness. Their hot sex in the hall had only been the start. From there, they'd gone into the shower, where Rip skillfully introduced her to the pleasures of making love on a slick surface. Then, barely dry and scarcely sated, they'd tumbled under the bedcovers. Between the stiff cotton sheets, they'd talked, teased and tormented until the party's start time approached and he'd left the suite to retrieve fresh clothes from the bags he'd left in his bike.

But no matter the music pulsing around her or the former classmates mingling in the open air of the rooftop bar, Erica couldn't shake the memories of lying in bed with Rip, sharing secrets and suckling each other to orgasm. He'd coaxed her into confessing precisely where she liked to be touched and tasted, for how long and with how much pressure. He'd fulfilled her every desire—then introduced her to a few new tricks that had sent her soaring over a sharp edge that had sliced away what might have been left of the past.

They'd gone too far to think of each other in high school terms anymore. They'd shared too much for her to pigeon-hole her attraction to him as simple lust or naughty nostalgia. Her weekend fling was threatening to turn into something new, adult and terrifying. And yet, she couldn't wait to find out where it would lead.

Aware that she was allowing her personal fantasies to get in the way of her job, Erica gave herself a shake. She took a few minutes to look over the hors d'oeuvres table, check in with the head waiter and consult the schedule. Then she joined a group of former cheerleaders drinking cosmopolitans and took a few minutes to catch up with them before greeting two classmates who'd once shared biology class with her and a former track star who had, not surprisingly, kept in incredible shape.

And through it all, she kept glancing at her watch. How long did it take a guy like Rip to throw on a pair of slacks and a shirt, comb his fingers through his luscious dark hair and stroll into the party like a returning hero?

No, not "like" a returning hero. He was a returning hero. In bed, he'd told her about his time in Afghanistan, about the foundation he ran for kids affected by crime, about his goal of drumming up some donations from his former classmates. Learning about who he was now had been fascinating and they'd only scratched the surface. He might have ridden out of town on a Harley, but who could have possibly expected him to come back as a man who was more exciting than he was before?

Just the thought of spending the rest of the night with

him, first at the party and then later in her suite, spiked her body temperature. She gravitated to one of the oscillating fans placed strategically around the rooftop bar and lifted her hair to invite the breeze onto the back of her neck. She closed her eyes and enjoyed the breeze while Shaw's band tripped through an instrumental version of the Kelly Clarkson hit that had been the theme of their prom.

"A Moment Like This."

"Now that's an invitation no man can resist," she heard Rip mutter right before he kissed the exposed spot on the back of her neck.

Startled, she jumped. He braced his hands on her bare upper arms.

"Don't," he whispered. "Don't be afraid."

"I'm not afraid," she lied.

Suddenly, she was terrified. Of what people would think—of what she feared would happen now that she was no longer just Erica Holt, Goody Two-shoes, and he wasn't only Rip Ripley, class scoundrel. It was one thing to enjoy the clash of differences in private. But in public? It was unthinkable.

And utterly, intensely invigorating.

"You're shaking," he said.

"I do that a lot around you."

She turned her head. Lord, his eyes were mesmerizing. Clear and blue and dancing with possibilities she wanted to experience so badly, her mouth watered.

"But not from fear," she clarified.

He spared the people around them a passing glance. "You don't care about what everyone is going to gossip about when they see us standing so close?"

"No," she said, meaning it—possibly for the first time in her life.

His grin was sin on a satin pillow—decadence with a dare. He was pulling her into a world she'd always wanted to live in…a world where she could do whatever she wanted simply because she wanted to.

"Want to dance?" she asked.

His gaze narrowed. "I don't dance."

"Oh," she said, twisting so that their bodies were practically pressed together. Somewhere behind her, she heard an increase in chatter, but she ignored it. It was easy to do with Scott Ripley staring down at her with unfiltered hunger in his eyes. "Did I just find something *you're* afraid of?"

"I'm afraid of stepping on your toes," he replied.

"You haven't seen the shoes I wear on a daily basis. Anyone who can pull off a four-and-a-half-inch-heeled Christian Louboutin platform pump for eight hours on a workday has feet of steel."

Taking his hand, she led him to the dance floor. As she'd asked Shaw to play slower, softer tunes during the first hour of the cocktail party to facilitate conversation, she knew that he'd segue from the Kelly Clarkson tune to something just as rhythmic and cadenced, something just as conducive to holding each other close and gently swaying to the beat.

As the party had just started, no other couples had yet to get on the dance floor. And when they stepped onto the custom-built tiles Erica had leased for the night, the ground underneath them lit to a soft, sensual blue.

If anyone had not been watching them before, they were now.

As RIP FOLDED ERICA into his arms, he felt every muscle in her body tense. Not from fear…from anticipation. They'd made love less than a handful of times, but he was already keying into her responses.

The way her breath caught when he snaked his hand onto the small of her back.

The way her nipples peaked against his chest.

The way she slid her tongue over lips that were moist with rich color just as her gaze darted to his mouth.

He hated that they were in public, not because he gave a damn about the chatter escalating around them. He just wanted to make love to her again.

"Now who's the one shaking?" she asked, glancing up at him with those liquid silver eyes.

"Only because it's taking all of my self-restraint not to grab your ass like I might have at the Susan Hawkins dance."

She laughed. "That's *Sadie* Hawkins, and I thought didn't dance."

"I don't. But you've got me doing all sorts of things I've never done before."

Her laugh was an explosion of doubt. "Like what?"

"Like wondering if we can slip behind that silk screen over there and get busy without anyone noticing."

"How is that different from all the times you lured girls under the staircase at school?"

"At school, I never cared if anyone noticed."

He spun her around, then braced his thighs to ensure that his attempt at distracting her didn't make her tumble off her high heels. But like a pro, she remained steady in his arms, her body as in tune with his as it had been first in the hall, then the shower, then the bed.

Only they hadn't made love in the bed, though he had gotten her off one last time. No man could lie around with a naked Erica Holt and not make sure she came undone. But now that he'd had time to recharge, he could think of nothing he wanted more than to carry her back up to her suite and finish what they'd started on a soft mattress. It was one thing to be inside her, but he wanted to be on top of her, covering her, enveloping her with every part of himself in a way they had not yet experienced.

"What are you thinking?" she asked.

Stunned, he twirled her again, hoping to distract her question.

"I'm thinking this dancing stuff isn't as hard as I thought."

"I don't know," she said, glancing around. "It's a little more difficult when everyone is watching."

"Do you care?"

"No," she answered. "It's just weird. I mean, haven't they ever seen two adults who are hot for each other before?"

"Not exactly like this," he replied, "especially since you always put out that 'do not touch me' vibe in high school."

"I did not put off that vibe," she said, smacking him lightly on the shoulder. "I had boyfriends."

"Is that what you called them?"

"What else would I call them?"

"Future gay best friends," he quipped. "Not that there's anything wrong with that."

She slapped him again, but her eyes sparkled with laughter. "None of my boyfriends in high school turned out to be gay. And I would know. I've planned four gay weddings this year alone, two for people I knew from school. And besides, I've been engaged more than once. I do know how to put out the welcome mat to the right guy."

"If they were the right guys, then why didn't you marry any of them?"

"That's a longer story than can be told during the course of one song."

Only one song had already become two. And if he was lucky, three or four or five. Despite his lack of enthusiasm for the act of dancing, Rip had no desire to let her go. He tugged her just a little closer and maneuvered them over to the left, hoping another couple would join them, make them less conspicuous so he could drop his hands a little lower on her waist without causing a scandal that would light up the alumni association's Facebook page.

"Well, unless you have a sudden desire for me to let you go, tell me your long story."

"I'm more interested in the future." She looked up at him, her eyes wide and expectant. "And the present."

If only lightening someone's emotional baggage was that easy. He knew better.

"You can't really move forward in life without understanding the choices you made in the past."

She snickered. "Is that your professional opinion, Dr. Ripley?"

He cleared his throat and took a chance in attempting a twirl. It was more of a spin, but since they didn't fall over, he considered the move a success.

"Actually, yes," he answered. "That is my professional opinion. I am a licensed psychotherapist."

Erica stopped dancing long enough to stare at him directly, as if she might spy a reflection of his degree in his eyes. She must have found what she was looking for because soon after, she eased back against his chest, first with her face away from him, then quickly shifting so that she could meet his gaze.

"I thought you ran a foundation."

"I do," he said. "But I worked with psychological services in Kabul before the end of my tour and that was my course of study once I got back. Does that freak you out?"

She snorted. "Of all the things about you, that's the least likely to freak me out. I told you earlier. I've been to therapy. And what's your professional opinion of me?"

"That you're hot."

"That's your personal opinion," she countered.

"No, actually, it's an irrefutable fact."

"And you think I was engaged three times but never made it down the aisle because—" She paused, leaving him room to fill in the blank.

He opted to take a different tack. "It's not uncommon for

women to gravitate toward men who won't consciously hurt them," he assured her. "And it's not a bad idea to pick the safe guys. They're generally underrated. But clearly, the ones you picked didn't meet your needs or you'd be married and dancing with one of them right now."

"Maybe I didn't meet their needs. You're assuming I did all the leaving at the altar."

"Didn't you?"

"I had the decency to break things off before anyone had put down deposits or sent out 'save the date' cards."

"But you did break all three hearts."

"Maybe one," she conceded, "but I didn't mean to. Do we ever mean to break hearts?"

Their gazes locked and he saw the glimmer of a challenge in her eyes—as if she was still holding him accountable for the emotions left over from him cutting off their friendship. He supposed he couldn't blame her. He hadn't meant to hurt her—just the opposite. But he had hurt her—and if he wasn't careful, he'd do it again.

"No, I don't think we mean to."

She shrugged and continued talking quickly. "I don't think the other two were that invested. One even invited me to his wedding to a mutual friend of ours six months after I returned his ring."

Rip grimaced, though he was thankful for the change in topic. "Ouch. Think he invited you for revenge?"

She laughed. "No, I think he just made a list of people he knew and I was on it."

"I'd like to think that if a woman dumped me after I shelled out the big bucks for a ring, I'd at least have the common decency to be pissed off."

"You'd never get engaged to a woman you didn't love entirely and completely."

"Now who's psychoanalyzing?"

The music ended and the people nearest the dance floor broke out into applause. For a horrified heartbeat, Rip thought they were clapping for their solo turn on the dance floor, but then he registered that while Erica had been revealing more about herself and her past to him than he ever imagined she would, Shaw Tyler had been singing. Damned if he'd recognized the song, but it had obviously gone over well with the crowd.

Erica pulled away, but not too far. Just enough so that he no longer had any valid excuse to keep his arms around her, which kind of ticked him off.

"That's going to be Shaw's next hit," she said, joining in the applause for a second before the band broke into an acoustic rendition of No Doubt's languorous reggae anthem, "Underneath It All." This time, a handful of couples straggled onto the dance floor.

"Shaw has hits?" he asked.

"Several, but for other artists. He's not very ambitious about performing. He just loves the music and sells songs to pay the bills."

Rip slid his hand around her waist and led her toward the bar. "So you know all that about Shaw, but you didn't know I what I did for a living?"

"Shaw plays a lot of my corporate gigs. We've kept in touch," she explained. "Did *you* keep in touch with anyone from school?"

"I'm in a fantasy football league with Jack Morris and Drew Billings. Chris Anderson looked me up last time he was in New York and Mick Wasterson worked with my unit outside Kabul when he deployed after West Point."

She raised her chin. "And here I thought when you left, you'd never look back."

"I don't think I really did look back," he said, sliding a finger under her chin to angle her face up to his, "not until now."

She met his bold stare. "And what do you see?"

"Honestly? I'm not sure. It used to be so clear. Now, not so much. Thanks to you."

# 7

ERICA LOST HER CHANCE to find out exactly what Rip meant when Kate dashed over and reminded her that she should have performed the official welcome announcements thirty minutes ago. She'd gotten so lost in their dance and private conversation that her normally innate sense of time had completely fallen away.

And that wasn't all. As Erica took to the stage, she felt stripped and exposed—but not in a bad way. She couldn't remember the last time she'd felt so authentic and real. When she accepted the microphone from Shaw, she wasn't worried about anything except powering through her official duties as quickly as possible so she could get back to Rip.

As she spoke, more than a few of her former classmates ping-ponged their stares between her and Rip. Her messages about the scramble golf tournament set for the morning and bar crawl event at lunch seemed muffled underneath the scrutiny. But Rip either didn't notice or he didn't care. Leaning against a column near the bar, he watched her with rapt attention, his gaze betraying his increasing and undeniable lust.

Forcing herself to focus on her digital tablet, she ran down the rest of the list of special events, focusing on the black-tie dinner and dance tomorrow night. She suddenly wondered if she and Rip would go together—if they'd last more than just this one night.

"So, everyone, if you need anything during your stay, be sure to contact Kate Schaffer," she said, gesturing toward her assistant, "and she'll take care of it. As your former senior class president, I hope you all have a fabulous time catching up with old friends and maybe make some new ones."

She glanced in Rip's direction and he responded with a wink.

The applause from the crowd spurred Erica off the stage, but she didn't get two steps off the dais when her former student council vice president, Lyn Young, bounced over. "You are the queen of great parties!"

They exchanged pecks on the cheek, but since Lyn went to the same gym that Erica did, they didn't have to try and fill in ten years worth of life experiences into a ten-minute chat. Of course, this left Lyn free to ask the question so many others wouldn't dare to.

"So, tell me. What's going on with you and Scott Ripley?"

Erica tried to look innocent. "We're just catching up, like everyone else."

"Honey, he looked like he wanted to strip you naked and do you on the dance floor. And I heard you rode up together on the back of a motorcycle and nearly ran down the head bellman. Trust me, no one else here is catching up that way."

With a shrug, Erica neither confirmed nor denied. She knew their secret was out, but she didn't have to reveal too many details.

Lyn narrowed her gaze. "I don't remember you ever being interested in him back at school."

"That was a long time ago," Erica said.

"Yeah, but he's still hot." Lyn's voice lilted with just enough wistfulness to remind Erica that sometime in sophomore year, Lyn and Rip had been an item—for about five minutes.

But then, he'd been "an item" with a lot of girls, but never for very long. Was he still the same way?

And did it matter if she was only in this for the weekend?

She managed to change the subject with Lyn, but didn't get very far in returning to Rip when another old friend, and then another, approached to join in the conversation. They complimented her on the reunion plans, asked about her parents, exchanged business cards and slyly attempted to pump information out of her about Rip before she made a viable excuse and extracted herself from the barrage. She found a quiet corner behind the bandstand and was nearly breathless so that she barely made a peep when someone grabbed her by the arm and tugged her behind a decorative wall that hid stacks of extra tables and chairs from view.

"Rip!"

He placed his hand over her mouth. "You want to get out of here, or what?"

The flash of mischievousness in his gaze zapped her sense of responsibility to smithereens. The fact that she should see the party through to the end dissolved under his heated gaze.

She nodded.

"Follow me."

He led her to the service elevator, but he didn't press the button for her floor, opting instead for the parking garage, a fact she only barely noticed when he drew her close and kissed her soundly.

"Where are we going?"

"I don't know. Out of here. We'll take my bike out this time."

The double doors dinged open and while she followed him into the darkened, underground structure, she had no desire to hop onto the back of a bike again. Part of her wanted to return to the party—the other part wanted to go back up to her suite. Either way, running off with Rip wasn't an option.

"Why?"

"What do you mean?"

She sidled up close to him. She could feel the hard press of his erection through his slacks. She could see the dark fire of desire in the pupils of his eyes. So why was he running off?

"Why are we running off when my suite is fifteen floors up?"

He started to pace, his hands streaking through his hair as pent-up energy created a tension in the air that Erica suspected had the capability to ignite.

"I have a sudden need to hit the open road."

She shook her head. "Don't you always?"

"No, that's just it, I don't. I mean, I haven't. Not since I left Chicago and joined the service. I settled down, got some focus, found my place. But I'm suddenly feeling like I need to hit the open road again. Come with me?"

"To New York?"

"What? No, just…out. I can't ask you to leave Chicago. I mean, can I? You just wanted a fling, right? A roll in the hay with the class bad boy to break yourself of your bad dating habits?"

Erica stepped back, her stomach dropping as if he'd said something insulting when what he'd said had been nothing but the God's own truth. That's exactly what she'd wanted from him—so why now did it sound like less than she deserved?

She forced a sensual grin. "Of course that's all I wanted. That's why I'm having trouble understanding why you want to go ride your bike when you could be upstairs riding me."

He nodded, but didn't move. His jaw clenched tight and his hands shoved into his pockets, he looked like a caged animal, one that Erica had no idea how to tame.

She approached him cautiously, hooking her hand around

his wrist and drawing his fingers to her mouth. She kissed his palm, then slid his warm flesh around her waist, then lower so that he cupped her buttocks. When she sidled even closer, he grabbed her tight and pulled her flush against him.

"You're like a drug," he said.

"Is that good or bad?" she asked.

"I'm not sure yet," he admitted, lifting her so that he could suckle the skin on her neck.

"Then take me upstairs so you can find out."

THE URGE TO RUN HAD BEEN wholly unexpected. Rip had watched Erica at the party, talking to friends, trying desperately, he knew, to get back to him so they could finish what they'd started earlier in her suite.

But what if he didn't want to finish? What if he didn't want this weekend to be both the start and end of the most exciting relationship he'd had in years, if ever?

He'd had a shot at her ten years ago. He'd been with enough girls to know when they were aching for him in a way that only he could soothe, but he'd let her go to save her the shame of being one in a long list of lovers who'd ultimately meant nothing to him except as an outlet for his discontent.

But he wasn't that same guy anymore. He'd come to terms with his crazy childhood and his parents' mistakes. He'd made amends by serving in the military and starting the foundation that helped kids like him who'd been affected by crime and criminals. All the justifications for keeping Erica Holt at arm's length had been stripped away, leaving nothing but the unbinding truth that she was, in a word, irresistible.

He pressed the button to recall the elevator. He held both her hands in his while they waited for the car to return, alternating between kissing her skin and smoothing her softness against his cheeks. When the bell dinged and the doors slid open, he led her inside and they rode up to her suite without exchanging another word.

She went in first. He locked the door behind him and watched from the hall as she stepped out of her shoes and pulled the tie that would unwind her form-hugging dress. For a split second, he imagined they weren't in a random hotel room, but were at an apartment. Maybe his. Maybe hers. The pull of familiarity socked him in the stomach and kept him from venturing farther into the room.

"Rip?"

"You're incredible," he said.

She smiled, but he could see her wariness just as she likely witnessed his.

"What's wrong?"

"I'm going to stay in Chicago."

He blurted it out. He wasn't thinking about repercussions or long-term plans. He was following his instincts, indulging his desires.

He was surprised when her eyes flashed and the corners of her mouth curved downward quickly before she tamped down whatever emotion she didn't want him to see.

"For the week, you mean?"

"I don't know," he said.

"Oh," she said.

She grabbed the sides of her dress and drew them close to her body, giving him the answer he sought. She was still banking on this affair being quick and easy and disposable. Any indication that he might want more from her and she shuttered away that bold, sensual woman he'd held in his arms on the dance floor and with whom he'd wanted to spend the whole night in bed. A couple of hours ago, he'd been fine with a brief affair. He had a full life in New York and no desire to get tangled up with a woman he would only disappoint when it was time for him to return.

Now, he'd disappointed her merely by floating the idea that he'd stay beyond the three-day reunion.

"Look," he said, glad he'd decided not to give up his room even though he'd had every intention of spending the whole of the weekend in hers. "It's been a long day. A lot is going on tomorrow. Maybe we should—"

"Yeah," she agreed before he could finish the thought, which was a good thing because he had no idea what to say next.

Luckily, he did know what to do.

He crossed the room and after searching her eyes for any sign of skittishness—and finding none—he kissed her in a way he never had before. Despite the dozens of times he'd pressed his mouth to hers over the course of the afternoon and evening, this was different. This kiss wasn't about passion or lust or reliving the glory days or making up for what he'd missed out on when he'd turned her down ten years ago.

This was about what he was feeling now.

He wanted more than a fling. He'd had flings. Hundreds of them. But from Erica, he wanted more. He always had. He simply had to figure out how to get it.

"I'll see you tomorrow?" she asked, her voice a whisper.

"I'll call you in the morning," he said. "We'll make plans."

He kissed her on the nose, then held her for a long minute, breathing in deeply to imprint the sweet mixture of her perfume into his mind.

Then he left.

He needed time to think. He needed space to work out a truce between his warring wants, needs and desires. Because as much as he'd wanted to make love to Erica tonight, first he had to figure out what it all meant—and if, in the end, he really had the strength to walk away.

# 8

A LONG TIME AFTER THE DOOR shut behind him, Erica dropped onto the mattress and tried to make sense of what had just happened.

One moment, Rip had hardly been able to keep his hands off her. Then, something had changed—shifted into territory she'd never expected to cross into with him. He'd hinted that he might stay in Chicago for more than just another two days and though the thought had given her heart a jolt not unlike an electric shock, the surprise had thrown her brain out of service. She hadn't known what to think or what to do. When he'd hinted that they should spend some time apart, she'd instantly agreed. She'd needed space. Time. Perspective.

No, she needed him.

Tying up her dress quickly, she grabbed her cell phone and called down to the front desk. She knew she was breaking a gazillion hotel policies by asking, but she used her influence and long association with the management to find out Rip's room number. He was only two floors below her, so she bolted down the stairs, too impatient to wait for the elevator.

She raised her fist to knock, then stopped herself.

What was she doing?

She had to think, plan, strategize. Rip wasn't like the men

she'd dated before, nor was he like the guys she'd agreed to marry. He was honest and clever and deeper than anyone had ever given him credit for. He'd see right through any of her bullshit the same way he'd always seen right through her.

What if she couldn't handle such authenticity? With Rip, she'd have no choice but to be her true and open self. He'd expect no less.

Luckily, she wanted even more.

The door opened.

"Erica?"

"I—"

"Is something wrong?" he asked, glancing down the hall.

He had his shirt off, but he was holding it in his hands, along with his key card. Was he going back up to the party or, hopefully, coming back to her?

"I don't want you to go," she admitted. "I mean, when the reunion is over, if you can stay, I want you to stay. I know I acted like I didn't a minute ago, but I was just surprised. I thought you wouldn't want to stick around."

He slid his hand around her waist and guided her inside. "I didn't think I'd want to stick around, either. But I do. I don't know for how long. I have a life in New York and I can't just walk away from it."

"I know," she said, sounding much more enthusiastic about his returning to the East Coast than she truly felt. "It's just..."

They were both stumbling over their words. Erica had so much she wanted to say, but wasn't sure how far to go or how fast. Luckily, he seemed to be suffering from the same affliction. He pulled the chair away from the corner by the window and invited her to sit down while he punched his arms into his button-down shirt and sat on the corner of the bed.

"This is weird," he said.

She laughed. "You do know how to cut to the heart of the matter."

"Job skill."

"No," she replied, shaking her head. "You've always had that ability. You see right through to the truth. If you'd kissed me all those years ago, I would have been just another notch on your bedpost."

"And I would have been just another guy you didn't marry."

"I don't think it would have gotten that far, do you?"

He leaned on his elbows, his head bowed. "Not likely."

"So what is it now? I had a good plan, you know. I considered every detail and took every possible outcome into consideration."

"All but one." He turned his face toward her and though his blue eyes met hers with startling intensity, she didn't look away.

"That you wouldn't want just a weekend fling."

He pressed his lips together and nodded. "Weird, right?"

"Yeah," she said with a shrug. "Sort of."

He scooted nearer and took her hands in his. She was shaking again, but to her surprise, so was he.

"Thing is, Erica, I've done the weekend fling thing. I got that out of my system a long time ago. I don't think I really realized it until you came riding into my life again, but I'm looking for something deeper this time. A real connection. A relationship."

"But I've done that, too," she said, glancing down at her hand and imagining each of the three diamonds she'd worn on her left ring finger. "And I've never made it work."

He leaned forward and kissed her knuckles. "You never tried with a guy like me, though."

She laughed. "This much is true."

As if he could no longer bear to be apart from her, he tugged her onto his lap. "I wasn't ready for a girl like you back in high school. You're serious and focused."

"Don't make me sound so boring."

"Don't sell yourself short, Erica. Never again. To a guy like me, you're almost too much woman to handle."

She arched a brow. "Only almost?"

"I'm up to the task."

He rounded his body to hers. She loved how her curves fit intrinsically into his, as if they'd been built for each other physically and spiritually.

He was a risk-taker, a rule-breaker, a game-changer. He'd certainly changed her expectations for this weekend—in a perfectly wonderful way.

"But you still live in New York," she pointed out.

"If that's the only distance we have to breach, I don't see the problem. We can be good for each other, Erica. I know it."

"You already have been good for me," she said. "I never would have indulged my inner vixen if you hadn't checked Yes on that RSVP box. It was a risk, but it almost never felt that way."

"I don't ever want you to be afraid with me. I won't hurt you," he promised.

Erica knew he couldn't really make any guarantees, but she also knew that he'd do everything in his power to stay true to his word.

"I know."

"I want to love you, Erica. Inside and out. Every. Delectable. Inch."

He punctuated each word with a kiss, his hands fumbling with the ties of her dress while she slid her hands into the folds of his unbuttoned shirt and moved the material aside. They'd stripped each other bare today in more ways than one, but in this case, Erica truly felt naked, as if he could somehow spy the tenderness of her heart through the paleness of her skin.

And yet, she trusted him. And even more importantly, she trusted herself. Her past mistakes had been the result of her playing it too safe, risking nothing and therefore, getting nothing in return. With Rip, she'd have to expose her every vulnerability and explore her deepest desires in order to find real happiness.

He'd be satisfied with nothing less.

And from now on, neither would she.

RIP RAN HIS HANDS INTO her hair and mussed the dark strands even as he bruised her mouth with his hungry lips. He tore back the sheets and coaxed her underneath with him, the rest of their clothes disappearing in a rustle of fabric over skin.

Her nipples were like candy, hard and sweet, and her moans of pleasure deafened him to all other objectives save manipulating her nipples so that the sounds intensified. She undulated beneath him, her hands tangled in his hair, her strangled cries of "yes," alternating with guttural groans of pleasure that sounded like his name.

The minute his sex pressed against hers, a wave of dizziness swept over him. This was what he wanted—what he needed. Erica, in his bed, joined with his body, connected to his soul.

"Oh, Rip," she cried.

He pressed a little deeper, his muscles aching from the restraint.

"Scott," he said, suddenly needing her to know him as completely as he wanted to know her. "Call me Scott. No one calls me Scott. No one but you."

"Scott," she repeated. "Yes, Scott, oh, yes. Right there."

He brushed kisses along her cheekbones, over her nose, then down to her chin. He wanted more than life itself to bury himself in her slick, hot sex, but he wanted to savor this just as badly.

Make it last.

For an hour. An evening. A lifetime.

He kissed her long and languorously. He'd been wild in

his youth, but he'd never made love without a thin barrier of latex around his cock and a wall of protection around his heart. Now, he had neither. The feel of her sex, the depth of her trust, was maddening and sweet and euphoric.

"You're so beautiful," he said.

He eased himself deeper, testing her sensitivity, which was keen and intense. She lifted her knees and tilted her hips so that he had no choice but slide in to the hilt, though he stilled when he reached the limit.

"You're torturing me."

He receded, then inch by thick inch, drove back in deeper, harder and perhaps, just a little faster. "No, I'm savoring. Trust me, Erica. I know what I'm doing."

"Oh, yeah, you do."

He watched her eyes, searching for any sign of reluctance or fear or regret. But he saw nothing but intense desire, edged with the glossy shine of total and utter faith. Each stroke, each touch, each kiss snapped a tether to his control and by the time she wrapped her legs around his waist and cried out his name, he was completely lost.

Or maybe he'd been lost for years. Maybe he'd finally found his way home. It wasn't every day that the Guy Most Likely to Ride out of Town on a Harley finally ended up with the Girl Most Likely to Steal His Heart, but it happened.

And now that he had her, he was certain he would never let her go.

\* \* \* \* \*

# COMING NEXT MONTH from Harlequin® Blaze™
## AVAILABLE JULY 24, 2012

### #699 FEELS LIKE HOME
*Sons of Chance*
**Vicki Lewis Thompson**

Rafe Locke has come to the Last Chance Ranch for his brother's wedding, but he's not happy about it. After all, Rafe is a city slicker, through and through—until sexy Meg Seymour *shows* him all the advantages of going country....

### #700 BLAZING BEDTIME STORIES, VOLUME VIII
**Kimberly Raye and Julie Leto**

Join bestselling authors Kimberly Raye and Julie Leto as they take you to Neverland—that is, *Texas*—in these two sizzling stories, guaranteed to make you want to do anything but sleep.

### #701 BAREFOOT BLUE JEAN NIGHT
*Made in Montana*
**Debbi Rawlins**

Travel blogger Jamie Daniels is determined to show sexy cowboy Cole McAllister that she's not like all the other girls—in and out of bed.

### #702 THE MIGHTY QUINNS: DERMOT
*The Mighty Quinns*
**Kate Hoffmann**

With just a bus ticket and $100 in his pocket, Dermot Quinn sets out to experience life as his immigrant grandfather had—penniless and living in unfamiliar surroundings. So the last thing he expects is to strike it rich with country girl Rachel Howe.

### #703 GUILTY PLEASURES
**Tori Carrington**

Former Army Ranger turned security expert Jonathon Reece always gets the job done. This time, his assignment is to bring in fugitive-from-justice Mara Findlay. Too bad the sexy bad girl outwits him at every turn...including in bed.

### #704 LIGHT ME UP
*Friends with Benefits*
**Isabel Sharpe**

Imagine walking into a photography studio run by the sexiest man you've ever seen and finding pictures...all of you. Jack Shea has captured her essence, but is Melissa Weber ready to bare even more?

# REQUEST YOUR FREE BOOKS!
## 2 FREE NOVELS PLUS 2 FREE GIFTS!

### ❦ Harlequin®

### *Blaze*™

### red-hot reads!

**YES!** Please send me 2 FREE Harlequin® Blaze™ novels and my 2 FREE gifts (gifts are worth about $10). After receiving them, if I don't wish to receive any more books, I can return the shipping statement marked "cancel." If I don't cancel, I will receive 6 brand-new novels every month and be billed just $4.49 per book in the U.S. or $4.96 per book in Canada. That's a saving of at least 14% off the cover price. It's quite a bargain. Shipping and handling is just 50¢ per book in the U.S. and 75¢ per book in Canada.* I understand that accepting the 2 free books and gifts places me under no obligation to buy anything. I can always return a shipment and cancel at any time. Even if I never buy another book, the two free books and gifts are mine to keep forever.

151/351 HDN FEQE

| | | |
|---|---|---|
| Name | (PLEASE PRINT) | |
| Address | | Apt. # |
| City | State/Prov. | Zip/Postal Code |

Signature (if under 18, a parent or guardian must sign)

### Mail to the **Reader Service:**
**IN U.S.A.:** P.O. Box 1867, Buffalo, NY 14240-1867
**IN CANADA:** P.O. Box 609, Fort Erie, Ontario L2A 5X3

Not valid for current subscribers to Harlequin Blaze books.

**Want to try two free books from another line?**
Call 1-800-873-8635 or visit www.ReaderService.com.

\* Terms and prices subject to change without notice. Prices do not include applicable taxes. Sales tax applicable in N.Y. Canadian residents will be charged applicable taxes. Offer not valid in Quebec. This offer is limited to one order per household. All orders subject to credit approval. Credit or debit balances in a customer's account(s) may be offset by any other outstanding balance owed by or to the customer. Please allow 4 to 6 weeks for delivery. Offer available while quantities last.

**Your Privacy**—The Reader Service is committed to protecting your privacy. Our Privacy Policy is available online at www.ReaderService.com or upon request from the Reader Service.

We make a portion of our mailing list available to reputable third parties that offer products we believe may interest you. If you prefer that we not exchange your name with third parties, or if you wish to clarify or modify your communication preferences, please visit us at www.ReaderService.com/consumerschoice or write to us at Reader Service Preference Service, P.O. Box 9062, Buffalo, NY 14269. Include your complete name and address.

HBI1B

*Montana. Home of big blue skies, wide open spaces...and
really hot men! Join bestselling author Debbi Rawlins in
celebrating all things Western in Harlequin® Blaze™
with her new miniseries,* **MADE IN MONTANA!**

*Read on for a sneak peek of
BAREFOOT BLUE JEAN NIGHT*

"OVER HERE," Cole said.

Jamie headed toward him, her lips rising in a cheeky
grin. "What makes you think I'm looking for you?"

He drew her back into the shadows inside the barn.
"Then tell me, Jamie, what are you looking for?"

A spark had ignited between them and she had the
distinct feeling that tonight was the night for fireworks—
despite the threat of thieves. The only unanswered question
was when.

"Oh, I get it," she said finally. "You're trying to distract
me from telling you I'm going to help you keep watch."

He lowered both hands. "No, you're not."

"I am. Rachel thinks it's an excellent idea."

He shot a frown toward the kitchen. "I don't care what
my sister thinks. You have five minutes, then you're marching right back into that house."

She wasn't about to let him get away with pulling back.
Not to mention she didn't care for his bossiness. "You're
such a coward."

"Let's put it this way..." He arched a brow. "How much
watching do you think we'd get done?"

She flattened a palm on his chest. His heart pounded as
hard as hers. "I see your point. But no, I won't be a good
little girl and do as you so charmingly ordered."

"It wasn't an order," he muttered. "It was a strongly

worded request. I have to stay alert out here."

"Correct. That's why we'll behave like adults and refrain from making out."

"Making out," he repeated with a snort. "Haven't heard that term in a while." Then he caught her wrist and pulled her hand away from his chest. "Not a good start."

"It's barely dark. No one's going to sneak in now. Once we seriously need to pay attention, I'll be as good as gold. But I figure we have at least an hour."

"For?"

"Oh, I don't know…" With the tip of her finger she traced his lower lip. "Nothing too risky. Just some kissing. Maybe I'll even let you get to first base."

Cole laughed. "Honey, I've never stopped at first base before and I'm not about to start now."

*Don't miss BAREFOOT BLUE JEAN NIGHT*
*by Debbi Rawlins.*

*Available August 2012 from Harlequin® Blaze™*
*wherever books are sold.*